DRIVEN

DRIVEN

Karen McShane

Commonwealth Books Inc.,

A Commonwealth Publications Hardback
DRIVEN
This edition published 2023
by Commonwealth Books
All rights reserved

Copyright © 2023 by Karen McShane
Published in the United States by Commonwealth Books Inc., New York.

Library of Congress Control Number: 2023026737

ISBN: 978-1-892986-52-8 (hardback)
ISBN: 978-1-892986-53-5 (e-pub)

No part of this book may be reproduced or utilized in any form or by any means, electronic or mechanical, including photocopying, recording, or by any information storage and retrieval system, without permission in writing from the publisher, except by a reviewer who may quote brief passages in a review to be printed in a newspaper, magazine or journal.

This work is a novel and any similarities to actual persons or events is purely coincidental.

First Commonwealth Books Hardback Edition October 2023.

PUBLISHED BY COMMONWEALTH BOOKS, INC.,
www.commnwealthbooks@aol.com
www.commonwealthbooksinc.com

Manufactured in the United States of America

Dedicated

to my husband, Jack and Chester. To Mum and Dad. To Hayley, Mike, Matt, Colleen, Ali and Cassie and to Naveyda, Ryker, Faith, Caiden, Karliah, Olin and Amelia.

One

Beth

    Beth tipped back her head, closed her eyes, and felt warm sun radiate onto her pale cheeks and forehead. She almost felt her freckles coming back to life after being dormant from the cold New York winter. No matter what strength SPF sun lotion she used, her freckles proliferated until they covered her face. It bothered her as a child, even though her mother assured her they were angel kisses. During adolescence, she used every lotion and potion to stop the freckles. She eventually gave up and resigned herself to the fact that when the sun came out, so did the freckles, and, for at least nine months of the year, she was a total freckle face.

    As she sat on the park bench, enjoying the first warm spring day of the year, she amused herself by watching people around her enjoy the local park. A little boy was determined to catch the ducks that waddled up and down the pond's bank. In the background was the sound of his mother yelling at him to leave the poor ducks alone, but he kept chasing them back into the water.

    The trees were beginning to turn green, as their buds sprang into life under the warm sun. The old, dead leaves that fell during the previous autumn covered the grass, but new blades pushed through the undergrowth as if to hide the past and promote the new season of spring. A very pregnant young woman walked down the path with an older woman, presumably her mother. The pair chatted and laughed as they passed Beth, neither looking over to acknowledge her.

A church bell rang twelve times, announcing lunchtime in Minneola, Long Island. People arrived at the park as if a train just arrived at a nearby station. Many looked like escapees from work, their business attire giving them away. Due to the limited number of park benches, some people found a dry piece of lawn, sat down, and claimed the area for the next hour.

Two men entered the park, both in their early forties, deep in conversation, their jackets thrown over their shoulders. They walked down the path toward Beth. The tall one with jet-black hair turned and smiled at her, as they passed the bench. Deep in conversation, he put his hand into his pants pocket to retrieve something, and a small piece of paper fell to the path.

Beth jumped to her feet and called, "Hold up!" She bent to pick up the piece of paper only to feel the heel on her right sandal break and throw her off balance. She ended up in a heap on the ground with the piece of paper in her hand, looking up sheepishly at the two men.

"You dropped this," she whispered, getting back to her feet.

Unfortunately, getting up wasn't as easy as anticipated. The taller of the two immediately offered his hand to help her up. She wobbled to her feet, smiling and nodding in embarrassment.

"Are you OK?" the tall man asked, concerned.

"I'm good, just a little embarrassed. No good deed goes unpunished, as they say. Anyway, my name is Beth McCann." She offered her hand.

"It's good to meet you, Beth. I owe you a new pair of sandals for rescuing my dry-cleaning receipt. I'm Anthony Vito. This is a buddy of mine, Joe Jackson."

Joe smiled, as Anthony continued.

"Can I help you get to your car or wherever you're heading?"

"I'm staying at the Park Hotel, just across the park. I'm sure I can hobble over there when no one's looking." She smiled.

"If it's not too forward of me, you could take my arm, and we can walk slowly to the hotel," Anthony offered.

Much to her horror, she felt herself blushing. "I'll be fine. No worries, but thanks for the offer."

Anthony's cell phone rang. He looked at the number and indicated he had to take the call, walking a short distance away to chat.

Beth took the opportunity to stand. "Give Anthony my thanks. Good-bye." She hobbled toward the hotel.

Beth was actually undercover FBI Special Agent Elizabeth McCleary from the Manhattan FBI satellite office of Melville, Suffolk County, Long Island. For the past three months, she and her team were looking into possible corruption within the Minneola City Hall.

Three months earlier, one of her confidential informants told her that gossip from the Nassau County Correctional Center was that the Minneola Chief of Police was involved in a cover-up of a recent drug case. Several wealthy drug dealers were recently convicted of selling drugs out of two homes in a low-income district of Minneola. During the investigation, more than one of the dealers claimed they had a financial arrangement with the manager of Woodbridge Rentals, who managed the two homes in the raids. Each said they paid the manager a kickback so he would ignore their activities.

When one of the dealers offered to expose the manager in return for a reduced sentence, he was told there was no evidence to substantiate his claim, and the police had no reason to believe the

| 3 |

manager was involved. Gossip at the Correction Center alluded to the fact that the manager, Sam Garillo, was related to the Minneola Chief of Police, Alfonse Paselli. Elizabeth didn't know who owned Woodbridge Rentals, because it was registered under an anonymous trust.

Elizabeth decided to take a closer look at the case in Minneola. Her investigations revealed that Police Chief Paselli was part of a large Italian family. His Grandmother Rosa immigrated into the U.S. from Naples, Italy. She gave birth to eleven children and took a few others off the streets of Little Italy in New York. The family moved to Long Island after World War Two and settled in Minneola.

As Elizabeth traced the family tree, it seemed that most of the Italian population of Minneola and its suburbs could be traced back to Grandma Rosa. It also seemed that the family had quickly immersed itself into the city's local government. Grandma Rosa could have boasted that her family included the Minneola City Inspector Anthony Vito, City Auditor Leo Catolina, District Attorney Maria Pasquale, and Police Chief Alfonso Paselli. During her investigation, Elizabeth also discovered that Sam Garillo, the former manager of Woodbridge Rentals, was also related to the late Grandma Rosa.

Chief Paselli had an exemplary record. He came up through the ranks of the police department to become chief five years earlier. He was a popular boss, deemed fair and approachable by his subordinates and was also very popular with the citizens. Visible around town, he was often seen on Saturday afternoons at the local supermarket with his wife of twenty-nine years.

City Inspector Anthony Vito, Alfonse Paselli's cousin, had a more interesting bio. At forty-one, he had worked at the City Inspector's office for fifteen years. Known as quick-tempered, he was divorced from his childhood sweetheart, Daniella, when the pressure of work and the stress of having twin boys sent him running into his secretary's arms.

Not only had that ended his marriage, it almost cost him his job when the secretary charged him with sexual harassment. She withdrew the allegations when compromising photos of her with another married man appeared in her mailbox one morning. Daniella took the boys, the house, child support, and a substantial alimony payment. Anthony temporarily moved in with his cousin, Sam Garillo, but Sam recently disappeared from town, leaving Anthony alone in the home.

Although Anthony was paying the mortgage on Daniella's home, child support, and alimony, he didn't seem short of money. He always wore fine designer suits, drove a late-model BMW, and ate at the finest restaurants. A popular man, he had no trouble finding a date.

Anthony's cousin, Sam Garillo, frequented exclusive nightclubs and bars around town before he disappeared. Never married, he was quite the ladies' man and never held a job for long. A lazy man, he was dependent on other family members. Ten years earlier, he was arrested for being part of an illegal gambling scam, but he avoided jail by doing community service instead.

City Auditor Leo Catolina, another cousin, was a devout Catholic who served on many committees at the Corpus Christi Roman Catholic Church. He was married to Maria, and their four boys were in Catholic school. Leo was known for always following the rules. His reputation was impeccable and somewhat boring.

Cousin Maria Pasquale, the DA for Minneola, lost her husband to cancer five years earlier and was a doting mother to her son and daughter. The children attended the same Catholic school as Leo's boys. Maria Catolina and Maria Pasquale were great friends. Catolina was a big support for Maria during her husband's illness and death. Maria Pasquale was another family member with an impeccable reputation who was well-liked by her associates at the DA's office.

Ironically, when Elizabeth investigated the three men indicted for running the drug houses, they were related, too. Grandma "Abuela" Teresa was born and lived in Guadalajara, the capital of the Western Mexican State of Jalisco. She also had eleven children and was involved in raising her great-grandson. She was a petite, religious woman with long, gray hair fashioned into a neat bun each morning. No one knew her true age, although some speculated she was over 100. Although old and bent over with scoliosis, she worked hard to raise her family.

In her younger days, she had chickens in the courtyard and a small garden filled with fruit and vegetables. The family lived in poverty, but the children never knew it and always ate and dressed well. Abuela Teresa was a self-taught seamstress. As her children and grandchildren grew into adults, there was little work available. Everything was controlled by local drug cartels.

Determined to escape the poverty, each male child became involved with the cartel. After basic training, they entered the U.S. illegally via the Rio Grande at the Mexico-U.S. border and were met by cartel members on the U.S. side, given fake identification, and driven to a safe house in New York State. As they acclimated into the American way of life, they became invisible, just more United States citizens.

Of the three men indicted for running drug houses, two were brothers, Carlos and Andreas Martinez. The third, a cousin named Miguel, shared the same last name. All three were related to Abuela Teresa. They operated two drug homes in the low-income district of Minneola.

In their testimonies, they claimed Carlos rented the first home from Woodbridge Rentals. Three months later, Sam Garillo, the manager of Woodbridge, sent an eviction notice to Carlos based on complaints of drug-related disturbances. Carlos, Andreas, and Miguel visited Sam Garillo in his office late one night, where Carlos told Sam they were offended at receiving the eviction notice and realized it must be an error on Sam's part.

They offered Sam a proposal that would make his life very easy or very difficult. Sam, who wasn't a very tough person, was offered $500 cash on top of each month's rent to let them stay in the home. Furthermore, they wanted another rental immediately, with another promised to them in the next few months.

With the second rental, Sam's extra cash payment would be $1,000, then, when they rented the third home, they would pay him an extra $2,000.

Sam said he would check with his cousin who owned the company, but that wasn't good enough. They wanted an immediate decision. Not wanting to know what the difficult option might be, Sam agreed. He added that complaints about their rental had already been sent to the Minneola Police Department.

Life was moving smoothly for Carlos, Andreas, and Miguel until Sam informed them he couldn't provide a third rental. They encouraged him to "unoccupy" another home.

Soon afterward, Sam disappeared from the Woodbridge Rental office, and the two drug homes were raided. Carlos, Andreas, and Miguel were charged with drug-related offenses and for the possession of sawed-off shotguns. Found with the guns was a list of names, including some names with a line through them. These names were of people who had recently disappeared or were murdered.

The list included the names of a prominent judge, local prosecutors, the chief of police and the DA, all presumably showing who the gang targeted next. All three vehemently denied the presence of the weapons and the list, suggesting that they were planted at the scene.

Carlos and Andreas, veterans of the prison system, were quickly incarcerated for drug possessions and intent to sell. No weapons charges were filed.

After reading all the files involving the case, Elizabeth knew there was little hard evidence of a cover-up, but her gut said something was absolutely wrong. She requested a meeting with the Assistant Special Agent in Charge, ASAC, Tony Kuertz of the Melville FBI satellite office, where she presented the case in great detail. He, too, shared her suspicions.

They decided Special Agent Elizabeth McLeary would go undercover to investigate the possible corruption in Minneola. She would become Beth McCann, a former employee of the City Auditor's office in West Chester, New York. She had left her job to care for her ailing parents, both suffering from Alzheimer's. Her father passed away one year earlier, and her mother passed away just three weeks ago.

The FBI office secured her a home to rent just outside Minneola in the Warsaw suburb. It was a semi detached building rented by two brothers who lived on the other side of the property. Joseph and Philip Jackson were contractors for City Hall and childhood friends of Anthony Vito. They used the property for their mother, who had Alzheimer's, but she was eventually moved to an assisted-living facility. Since the rental home wouldn't be available for two weeks, Beth temporarily lived at the Park Hotel. Once she settled into her new rental, she would seek employment at City Hall.

Two

Anthony

Anthony Vito was Grandma Rosa's favorite. Although she didn't speak much English, she interjected English words into a sentence of Italian. As a child, Anthony became accustomed to Grandma Rosa pinching his cheeks and kissing his forehead. She often grasped his hand to slip him a dollar bill when no one saw. In turn, he doted on her. She was the first one he ran to after school to give a big hug. He sat on her sofa and told her everything about his day, describing his friends and teachers. She shook her head and wagged a finger when he related anything bad, and she laughed hysterically when he did. It was as if she understood all his words.

Grandma Rosa was the only one he allowed to cut his hair, and he often told her his dreams of the future when he sat in her "barber's" chair. After dinner, Grandma Rosa sent him to the corner shop to buy ice cream for everyone. The best part of that job was being allowed to keep the change.

He lost his grandmother just before he graduated from high school, and he was devastated. He missed most of the fun activities after graduation. He didn't attend prom and wouldn't go to the graduation ceremony until his mother sat him down and told him his grandma would be disappointed if he didn't attend. He agreed only when his mother allowed him to carry one of Grandma Rosa's favorite brooches in his pocket when he received his diploma.

Instead of attending college, Anthony did odd jobs for family members. He also worked at his cousin's auto body shop occasionally. He hated the dirt and grease of that job and soon found himself running errands part time for the City Inspector at City Hall. Mr. McDouglas, the inspector, was the father of his buddy, Mick, at school.

Anthony liked working for Mr. McDouglas, because he trusted Anthony to run important documents across town. With the money he earned, Anthony bought his first suit and presented himself the following Monday morning at Mr. McDouglas' desk to ask for a promotion.

Trying to keep a straight face, Mr. McDouglas replied, "Someone as well dressed as you shouldn't be running errands."

Somehow, Mr. McDouglas got Anthony an internship with the Inspection Office at City Hall. Anthony hoped Grandma Rosa was looking down at him from heaven to see his success.

Over the following five years, Anthony rose to the position of Assistant City Inspector, and he completed college courses in the evenings. During that time, he proposed to Daniella, his childhood sweetheart. The large wedding was planned by the entire family, a typical Italian affair that lasted seven days.

Anthony couldn't wait to get back to work and a more normal life. Soon after the wedding, Mr. McDouglas suffered a stroke and went into rehab at the local hospital. After doing the job for five years, Anthony officially stepped in as Acting City Inspector. Although the position lasted over five months, Anthony resisted updating the antiquated system Mr. McDouglas used out of respect for his boss.

One morning, the Mayor of Minneola called Anthony into his office. "Mr. McDouglas has agreed to retire as long as you take his position. You'll have to go back to school to get a diploma in Building and Construction, but you can take over immediately." The mayor knew Anthony had been doing the job well and showed a lot of enthusiasm.

Anthony immediately began updating the city's antiquated computer system to link code and enforcement policies with all the other aspects in the City Inspection office. It was a thankless task that took months to transfer the old handwritten records into the computer. During that time, Daniella became pregnant with twin boys. She had a difficult pregnancy and spent most of the nine months on bed rest.

Tired and bored, she called her husband at work to pass the time. He tried to keep her happy while updating the computer system and staying up-to-date on inspection jobs, but it was an impossible task. He was already sleep deprived when the twins Mario and Matteo arrived prematurely. Small but strong, the boys were out of NICU in two weeks and went home with Daniella and Anthony. He begrudgingly took a week off work but hired a secretary to continue updating the computer system while he was away.

Anthony loved being a father and enjoyed every daylight hour with his boys, but the nighttime hours were difficult. Daniella was breastfeeding and couldn't keep up with the demand from the twins. She pumped milk as they rested and stored it in the refrigerator. Daniella became exhausted and needed sleep in order to watch the boys during the day.

The first week, Anthony dutifully fed the boys through the night with pumped milk from the fridge. By the time he returned to work, he was exhausted. Unfortunately, Daniella felt he should continue feeding during the night, which not only left Anthony physically exhausted, but he also came to resent his wife. He began to work late deliberately, so he could nap before going home. His temper flared during the day at the office and even worse at home with Daniella.

He began dreading going home. Susie, his secretary, found him slumped over his desk one morning, fast asleep. His wrinkled clothes revealed he hadn't gone home the previous night. She gave him the key to her apartment and told him to take a nap and shower, while she brought him a clean shirt, underwear, and socks. Nodding like a child, he left.

A few hours later, Susie arrived with the clothing and cooked him breakfast at two in the afternoon. Anthony was so grateful, he began visiting her apartment twice a week to catch up on sleep. She started laundering his clothes, so he always had something to wear when he woke up from his naps.

One night when Anthony went home, Daniella accused him of having an affair, because a friend told her she saw him going into a woman's apartment. He tried to explain the truth, but she refused to listen. Their screaming match culminated in Anthony tossing some clothes into a bag and walking out.

He arrived at Susie's apartment. Despite having a key, he knocked before entering. Surprised at seeing him, she let him in.

Anthony explained what happened and asked to sleep in her guest bed. Susie busied herself cooking dinner, while he showered. They sat at the small kitchenette table and ate in silence. Anthony kept going over the conversation with Daniella. Susie respected his privacy.

They went to their respective bedrooms, but even though he was physically and mentally exhausted, Anthony couldn't sleep. He crept into the living room and turned the TV on low. Within minutes, Susie joined him, also unable to sleep. She poured a large brandy for both of them.

After their third glass, they giggled like school kids. Anthony slurred a word, and Susie laughed hysterically., He remembered his grandma laughing like that when he told stories, many of which she didn't understand.

He put an arm around Susie and told her about his beloved grandma. As the two of them laughed, Anthony turned and kissed Susie. She responded passionately

The following morning, they awoke in Susie's bed with throbbing headaches. She slipped out of bed and showered while Anthony lay there, realizing the implications of what just happened.

Susie came back into the bedroom wrapped in a towel. Anthony apologized to her and said they wouldn't be intimate again. He regretted what happened. Susie walked back into the bathroom, while Anthony dressed hastily and left.

Anthony confronted Daniella at home and explained what happened the previous night, begging for forgiveness.

"Pack your bags and get out," she said calmly. "Our bond is broken. I'll never trust you again."

He packed and drove to Sam Garillo's house, asking if he could stay there until he was more organized.

Adding to Anthony's despondency, Susie went to the mayor's office and accused Anthony of sexual harassment. Anthony was placed on administrative leave, while Daniella hired an attorney to start divorce proceedings.

Anthony, sinking into deep depression, barely left Sam's house. His first cousin, Chief Alfonse Paselli, came to visit the two

| 13 |

men after investigating the past of Anthony's former secretary, Susie Blake. After setting some photos on the table, the chief walked out.

The pictures showed Susie in compromising positions with another man. Under the photos were some court documents about the case of Susie Blake v. Jacob Mullin, held in Suffolk County, New York, where Susie accused her boss at the time of sexual harassment.

The jury found the relationship was consensual and ruled in favor of Jacob Mullin.

Sam took the papers. "Let me handle this, and don't ask any questions."

The following day, the mayor's office called and asked Anthony to come in, where he was told the charges against him had been dropped, and Susie resigned.

"I won't tolerate such a scandal at City Hall again," the mayor warmed. "The next time you're out, no questions asked."

Grateful to still have his job, Anthony didn't contest the divorce, going against his attorney's advice. Daniella ended up with full custody of the twins, the house, child support, and a large alimony payment.

Determined to stay out of trouble, Anthony buried himself in his work and completed the update of the city's computer system. Sam rarely saw him at the house except for brief meetings late at night or first thing in the morning.

Three

Sam

Sam Garillo, great-grandchild of Grandma Rosa, grew up as a privileged only child who wanted for nothing. He didn't do well in school and rebelled against the discipline. His parents blamed the public school system and placed him into private schools, where he did no better. The wealthy culture he found, however, appealed to him. He hobnobbed with elite families and blamed his parents when they couldn't keep up the financial side of his after-school activities. Disappointed with the car his parents bought him for his seventeenth birthday, he refused to drive it to school.

Once out of school, he depended on his extended family, because he didn't want to start any career at the bottom. Lazy and insolent, Sam was taken under Anthony's wing, who tried to teach him the value and pride of earning his own money. He set Sam up with a buddy who owned several Manhattan nightclubs.

Sam became a popular barman at Club 22 who loved the attention from single women he met. Most nights, he stayed in the city with a colleague, usually returning to Long Island once a week. He had a small apartment in Minneola compliments of his parents when he graduated from high school.

Every penny Sam earned at the club was spent. He knew his estranged parents would pay the real-estate taxes on his apartment, and his utility bills were low. He dressed well, ate most meals at the club, and lived the high life. Each night he met a different woman, some of whom he went home with after his shift depending on his mood. With his access to so many women, the one woman he shouldn't have pursued was the one who cost him his job and almost his life.

Jeff Sykes graduated with Anthony and owned four nightclubs in Manhattan. Anthony talked to him several times about giving Sam a job as a barman. Veronique, Jeff's girlfriend, was well known in the New York City clubs. A stunning French-Canadian model, her face was on almost every magazine cover. In television interviews, she was aloof and unapproachable, but at the nightclubs, she was friendly and sociable with the staff.

Sam was completely enthralled by her. She came to the bar early in the evening and chatted with him and the rest of the bar staff. As soon as the club became busy, she found Jeff, and the two left for the other clubs he owned. Sam was convinced Veronique was as interested in him as he was in her.

On Sam's night off, he sat at the bar to enjoy free drinks. It was late, and he was ready to leave until he saw Jeff and Veronique at the end of the bar. Jeff took a phone call and walked away to escape the loud music.

Full of Dutch courage, Sam walked over to Veronique, who recognized him and smiled. He took Jeff's vacant seat and leaned forward as if to speak to her over the loud music. As she leaned toward him, he kissed her passionately.

Veronique pulled away abruptly, losing her balance on the bar stool and falling with arms flailing. She grabbed onto Sam and pulled him down with her to the floor.

As they fell, camera flashes lit up the bar and brought even more attention to their plight. Jeff, a large security officer in tow, ran toward them, while a woman shouted, "That man tried to kiss her!"

Veronique, in agony, bled from a head wound. Her right leg was twisted and broken where Sam landed on her. The security officer lifted Sam with one arm and removed him from the scene, as Jeff called 911. The bar staff cordoned off the area and waited for the paramedics and police.

Veronique was taken to the hospital, while Sam was escorted to jail. His intake picture showed two black eyes and a broken nose.

Veronique was diagnosed with a femur fracture, a large scalp laceration, and a concussion. She had surgery the same night. Sam was charged with sexual assault and physical assault and given bond. Anthony paid his bail and drove him to Sam's apartment in Minneola. The charges were later reduced, and Sam received a large fine and community service, because it was his first offense.

Four

Phil and Joe Jackson

Phil and Joe Jackson grew up next door to Anthony and his family. Their mother was a devout Irish Catholic, and their father was a non-practicing Protestant. Despite the rivalry between the Italians and the Irish, the two families were close and supported each other during times of joy or sadness. Phil, Joe, and Anthony were like brothers. When they were in trouble, Grandma Rosa chastised each of them in Italian with a few English words tossed in. She was the only grandma Phil and Joe knew. They loved her, even though Anthony was her favorite.

Joe Jackson, Senior, died before the boys were teenagers. He worked nights at the steel mill and suffered a fatal accident with one of the machines. The details were withheld from the boys for their sake. Their mother never got over the loss and became clinically depressed for years.

Anthony's family took responsibility for the boys. They spent more time at the Vito house than at their own home. However, every night they went home to sleep in their own beds.

As the Jackson boys grew older, their mother became more withdrawn. Once they left for college, she moved in with her sister in another state. Later, she was diagnosed with Alzheimer's and lived in an assisted-living facility, sharing a room with her sister. Each weekend, one of the boys drove 200 miles to visit her.

Phil and Joe attended the local college, where Joe studied construction, and Phil studied business. It seemed natural after both graduated to go into business together. Anthony, their best friend, worked in an auto body shop, which he hated, while they were in college. They often discussed the idea of going into business together after the brothers finished college. Although that didn't happen, they created a working relationship.

Joe and Phil opened a construction company called Jackson Construction. Joe ran the construction side, while Phil covered all administrative duties. Once Anthony became the new City Inspector, he needed to get his diploma in Building and Construction. Joe worked tirelessly with Anthony to teach him the trade. Without Joe's help, Anthony didn't think he would have achieved his diploma.

To repay Joe, Anthony got them to bid and become the predominant city contractors. With inside information from Anthony, Joe and Phil beat all the competitors' bids and were awarded the contract.

Five

Joe and Phil couldn't keep up with the work assigned by the city. Although they hired staff, they soon found out if they wanted things done properly, they had to do it themselves or check everything twice. Joe settled with four reliable workmen and still had to subcontract at times. Phil found a great secretary, leaving him more time to run the business. There was no marketing or advertising needed, but the city's paperwork was a full-time job.

The mayor introduced a pilot program called RESCUE, Residents Emergency Services Caring for the Underprivileged Elderly, to assist those elderly residents still living at home. The program proved very successful in the city where the mayor previously worked. It specifically addressed emergencies and code violations posing threats to the elderly's health and safety, affecting their ability to remain at home. The assistance, paid by the city, was targeted to enable seniors to continue living independently in their own homes.

Once a RESCUE request came in, Anthony inspected the property to determine if the case met the criteria. The inspector ordered the work through city contractors, checked the work, and submitted the paperwork for payment to the city, so the contractors would be paid.

RESCUE tripled the workload for Jackson Construction. Even though they hired more staff, they slowly fell increasingly behind on their work schedule, leading to delays in the program. Written complaints from the public were submitted to the mayor's office, which were rerouted to Anthony with a handwritten note from the mayor stating *Unacceptable.*

Frustrated, Anthony arranged a meeting with Joe and Phil at a local bar. To catch up with the backlog, the three agreed to apply what they called a "Band-Aid" to the waiting RESCUE cases until they were caught up. They would go to those jobs to finish the work once work slowed. The money received from the city in those cases would be kept in a separate account to fund outstanding work.

Although it seemed like a watertight plan, the problem was that demand never slowed. Work was getting done on time, but there was never time to complete it. Phil became concerned with the amount of money building up in their "work still to be done" account. The other issue was that Joe and Phil were working seven days a week to keep up, which stopped their weekend visits to their mother at the assisted-living facility. Staff recently advised them that their mother would soon need full-time nursing home care.

They scrambled to find a nursing facility closer to home, booking appointments to view them, then having to cancel due to work commitments. Eventually, the assisted living staff placed their mother in their own nursing home facility in the same location.

Anthony and the brothers had another meeting. Anthony arrived feeling annoyed, because Daniella yelled at him over the phone for an hour saying the twins needed a nanny. He was already struggling financially to pay the alimony, child support, and mortgage on the home she lived in, along with his own expenses. He was still living with Sam and had almost no money of his own.

Joe and Phil were upset due to the sudden out-of-state nursing home placement. Once Phil began talking, the worries paled into insignificance, however, when he revealed the balance of the monies in the "work to be done" account had reached $500,000.

Anthony and Joe were shocked, and they realized they faced an impossible situation. It wasn't possible to reverse the clock. They didn't have the time or the manpower to finish the Band-Aid jobs and continue with the amount of new work waiting. If the mayor found out about their situation, Anthony would be fired, and Jackson Construction would lose its city contract. There was also the question of whether they had acted within the law.

As Anthony stared at the bank balance, he recalled Daniella's words that he was a terrible father who couldn't take care of his own children. He told the brothers, and they told him how some extra money would allow them to purchase a small home for their mother nearby, with twenty-four-hour nursing care.

By the end of the meeting, there was no doubt their plans were unlawful. The Band-Aid accounts would be considered finished. The money in the spare account would be split three ways. Due to the overwhelming number of new cases, it was decided that Anthony would review them to see which ones he could deny to the homeowners but still have them approved by City Hall. That would allow him to file the paperwork to state the jobs were finished and inspected, which would trigger payment to Joe and Phil.

The money from those jobs would be split three ways. Each had to find a way to hide his portion of the funds or launder them into legitimate income. Anthony would find a vacant home, owned by the city, for Mrs. Jackson, and would undervalue it. The brothers would pay cash for it.

Although a line had been crossed, the solution allowed them to move forward and continue, at least on paper, to meet the demands of the RESCUE program. Each of them supported the plan and swore not to tell anyone about it.

Anthony managed to secure the house next door to Joe and Phil's home for their mother. It was the perfect solution for them. Anthony undervalued the property, they bought it, and remodeled it into a perfect sanctuary for their mother. Anthony soon realized the city had many vacant homes left empty after elderly people died. It seemed the perfect solution to launder his ill-gotten gains.

He set up an anonymous trust that opened a business called Woodbridge Rentals. He made Sam Garillo, his cousin and roommate, the manager. As City Inspector, Anthony would undervalue the vacant home, and Woodbridge Rentals would purchase it with cash. After minimum repairs, the house was rented to low-income families under Section Eight housing. That way, the city paid rent to Woodbridge Rentals as legitimate income.

Daniella got the nanny she wanted, who was paid in cash each week. Anthony became the perfect daddy again. He bought himself a beautiful home in the next county and rented a small loft in the city to live in during the work week.

Anthony's family knew about the Woodbridge Rental business and were impressed by the way Anthony took Sam under his wing. Sam had gainful employment and a purpose. He also found his niche. He enjoyed the benefits of a regular paycheck and did well managing the business.

At Easter, the family traditionally met to go to church, and then they enjoyed Easter dinner together at the family home. Each year, the crowd grew larger, as more babies were born into the large Italian family.

Joe and Phil became part of the tradition. Anthony decided there were too many bodies to put into a small family home, so he made arrangements with Father Mulcahy to use the church hall after services. The priest was delighted to attend.

Every invitation to the catered event was accepted. Over eighty families came, and Joe and Phil even brought their mother for a short time.

After the event, a few family members walked back to the family home to enjoy a brandy. Anthony and his cousin, Police Chief Alfonse Paselli, sipped brandy and smoked cigars, as they reminisced about the past. Alfonse was obviously very touched about Anthony's employing Sam at Woodbridge and voiced his concerns for Sam before he was given the job.

"He's been a godsend," Anthony said. "He's practically running the business himself. He hired a great secretary, and business is booming."

"There have been several unsubstantiated complaints about one of the Woodbridge homes dealing in marijuana. We investigated, but we didn't find anything."

Anthony almost dropped his cigar. He couldn't understand why Alfonse hadn't told him earlier or why Sam hadn't mentioned it.

The following day, Anthony went to the Woodbridge Rental office and spoke to Emily, Sam's new secretary, although the plaque on her desk read *Administrative Assistant.*

"Hi," Anthony said. "I'm Anthony Vito, the owner, and I've heard there have been complaints and police activity concerning a rental."

"Yes. The police came to the office and searched the home in question, but they found nothing."

As the conversation continued, Sam came in, drenched from the rain.

Feeling irate, Anthony told Emily, "Take a coffee break."

When he was alone with Sam, he berated him furiously.

"I'm the manager," Sam said. "I handled it appropriately. I didn't think you needed to be involved."

Red in the face, Anthony seemed ready to explode. Putting his hands on his head, he walked outside into the rain to cool off. When he returned, he told Sam to check the house again.

"If there's any sign of drugs, you have to evict them immediately," Anthony added.

"I'll call you and let you know what I find."

"If anything like this happens again without letting me know, heads will roll." He stormed out.

Sam never saw his cousin act that way before. Anthony could be a hothead at times, but the sheer anger he displayed was completely new.

Sam asked Emily for the file on the rental and drove across town to the address. It was in a poor neighborhood, with wet children's toys and bikes strewn on brown grass enclosed by a chain-link fence. There were no cars in sight.

Sam knocked without getting an answer, although he heard children's voices inside. He knocked again, and eventually, he heard several locks turning until the door opened to the limit of the security chain, and a young Hispanic woman peered out.

Sam introduced himself and asked to come inside. It was obvious she didn't understand English, because she shrugged and closed the door.

Sam walked around the side of the house to peer into a kitchen window. The rain had stopped, and he saw a small scale, some baggies, and white powder on the kitchen table.

He returned to the office and had Emily prepare a notice of immediate eviction for the home and notified City Hall. He contacted his cousin, Alfonse, and told him about it, adding, "I never saw Anthony so angry before."

"I'd be angry, too, if drug dealers lived in one of my homes. Shape up and don't let Anthony down again."

Three days later, Sam was finishing work in the office after Emily left for the evening. He heard a bell indicating someone came through the front door. Within seconds, he saw three large Hispanic men walk into his office.

The front door locked with a loud click, as a fourth man walked in. "Sit down," he ordered Sam.

He wore a black suit, white shirt, and thin black tie. The others wore black jeans and black sleeveless T-shirts that revealed many tattoos on their arms. All had shaved heads. One had large brass knuckles on his right hand, another had a revolver stuck into his pants pocket, and the third had a chain.

The man in the suit wandered around the office, opening drawers and flicking through papers piled on top. Finally, he faced Sam and placed his hands on the arm rests of Sam's chair until their faces were very close.

"Rico, give Mr. Sam here what we brought him."

"Yes, Boss." Rico tossed the eviction notice onto Sam's knees.

"Mr. Sam, you obviously made a big mistake. You see, I found this attached to my babe's front door. Did you make a mistake, Mr. Sam?"

Before Sam could reply, Rico lunged at him. "Answer him, Motherfucker!"

Sam immediately wet his pants.

"Oh, no, Rico." The boss grinned. "You made Sam piss his pants. Now that wasn't very nice, was it, Mr. Sam?"

The boss sat on Sam's desk and stared up at the ceiling, as he spoke. "It seems we have a predicament. We want to stay in the home, and you want us out. Definitely a predicament. So, Mr. Sam, you have a very big decision to make, one that will make me happy or one that will make me very sad.

"You can either continue with the eviction notice and make me sad. That would make Rico very sad, too. Or you can make me happy and let me stay. If you let me stay, I will continue to sell my drugs from my babe's home, and you will convince your police chief cousin that nothing is going on at that house. You will also tell me if you hear of any raids in the area from the chief. In return for this kindness, I'm willing to pay a little more rent directly to you. Do you understand, Mr. Sam?"

Sam nodded slowly.

"I think he understands, Boss." Rico laughed.

"Now, Mr. Sam, this is the good part. Are you listening? I will give you $500 a week in cash for your generosity. That's a pretty good offer, don't you think?"

Sam nodded.

Rico lunged at him again. "I didn't hear you, Mr. Sam. What did you say to the boss?"

"Yes. Yes, I understand." Sam's face was white. He turned his head to one side and vomited over the side of the desk, narrowly missing the boss.

"Look at that, Boss. Mr. Sam isn't feeling so good. Perhaps he should go home to bed."

"OK, Mr. Sam," the boss said. "It was nice to meet you. Make sure you keep your end of the bargain. Otherwise, I won't be able to stop Rico from visiting you. He loves to visit new friends, don't you, Rico?"

Rico smiled, revealing a mouth filled with gold teeth. He clapped his knuckles together, grinned, and turned, following the others from the office.

"Say hi to Miss Emily for me, won't you, Mr. Sam?" Rico asked, as he walked out the front door.

Sam vomited again before he made it to the front door to lock up. He watched through the window as the car carrying the Hispanic gang pulled out of the driveway and onto the road.

After running to his car, he drove home, trying to call Anthony on his cell, but there was no answer. As he drove, he wondered if Anthony knew something about the gang. Maybe that was why he'd been so angry when he last visited.

Sam didn't know what to do next. He didn't want to call Alfonse, because, for the first time in his life, Alfonse was proud of him.

Once home, Sam downed a half bottle of brandy and took a hot bath. He discarded his soiled clothes, hoping some of the memory of that encounter would go with them. He kept vacillating over whether to tell Anthony. He didn't want to feel his wrath again, and he didn't want to lose his job.

Despite the brandy, he was still sober. In that state of mind, he decided he would cooperate with the gang and not tell anyone. He would call Alfonse the following day and ask him to notify him, not Anthony, if there were any more complaints about rentals and tenants.

Sam took the following day off, but called Emily to say he met the occupants of the rental they intended to evict. "Cancel the eviction order. It's been sorted out."

"Are you feeling OK? I saw the vomit in your office."

"I must've eaten something bad. I had to leave in a hurry."

As promised, an envelope with $500 was dropped off at the office each week. If Alfonse called to report any suspicious activity in the city, Sam passed the news along to the gang. It was an unlikely symbiotic relationship that seemed to work. Anthony was happy with Sam again and added six more rentals to the company in the following three months.

Summer heat arrived before Sam saw Rico again. The office door was propped open to allow some of the sweltering air to escape. Sam heard Emily talking to someone, and she began laughing.

Sam entered the office and froze at the sight of Rico.

"Here he is, Rico," Emily said. "I told you Sam would be back soon. I had no idea you two knew each other. I'll leave you two alone. Thanks again, Rico, for helping my mom last week with that flat tire. You were so sweet to put on the spare for her. She wants you to come over some night for dinner. You will won't you?" she placed her hands together as if praying.

"Of course I will, Emily. I wouldn't miss dinner with Marigold and you. Perhaps Sam could join us?" Rico looked at Sam, who furiously shook his head.

"Let's go into your office and chat," Rico said.

Without speaking, Sam walked into his office, followed closely by Rico, who shut the door behind them.

Rico walked around Sam's desk and sat in the chair, while Sam remained standing.,

"Aw, come on, Sam. Can't we be friends? We're business associates now." He gave Sam a golden smile.

Sam smiled thinly.

"It seems business has been quite lucrative since our last meeting," Rico said. "We owe a lot to you, My Friend. The boss asked me to come down to talk more business with you. We need another house to sell from, not too close to the one we already have. We need to spread our wings, as they say."

"I don't have any other homes vacant," Sam replied sheepishly.

"Come on, Sam. You're the big boss here. Make one vacant. You seem good with eviction notices. You better keep the boss happy. You have one week. For your generosity, we'll increase your bonus to $1,000 a week. I'll be back next week for the keys."

Rico left the office and told Emily to call him to set up the dinner.

Sam walked slowly into the front office.

"My God, he's gorgeous," Emily said. "Such a man. I wonder if he's seeing someone."

Without replying, Sam returned to his office and pulled the logs of the rentals they had. Finding one ten miles from the first, he called Emily on the office phone.

"You need to prepare an eviction notice for Property 42."

"What's the reason?" she asked.

"Numerous neighbor complaints of noise violations."

"No kidding? They seem like such a nice couple."

Rico picked up the keys as promised one week later and left Sam an early bonus of $1,000 in cash. He also made a date with Emily before he left.

Sam felt sick. The situation was getting to be more than he could handle. Soon, however, he appreciated the extra $500 he was getting, telling himself it was a fair payment for what he was going through.

The family's Memorial Day picnic was scheduled for the beginning of May. Everyone was invited to the local state park where Anthony reserved the pavilion. All brought dessert dishes, and Perry, the local BBQ king in town, brought his smoker and thrilled everyone with ribs, chicken, and pulled pork.

Although the state park didn't allow alcohol, Anthony arranged for a soft drinks bar with alcohol hidden under the table. "Virgin" daiquiris, margaritas, and martinis made everyone giddy. Even a couple cops stopped by, buddies of Anthony's, and enjoyed a few drinks and ribs. Anthony sat in his lawn chair and watched Sam, sitting alone, downing drink after drink. Finally, Anthony moved his chair beside Sam's.

"You may want to slow down, Buddy. This is a family affair. We don't want anyone falling over at an alcohol-free party, do we?"

Sam glared at him. "I can handle it. I won't embarrass you."

"What's going on, Sam? This isn't like you. What's troubling you?"

Sam picked up his glass and walked away, and Anthony immediately followed.

"I'm good, Anthony," Sam said. "Back off. I'm going home."

As Sam walked off, Anthony stared speechless.

Alfonse walked up. "What's wrong with Sam?"

"I have no idea. Something's bothering him."

"Perhaps it's women trouble."

"I hope you're right."

The two men returned to the picnic.

Emily also noticed a change in Sam and found empty liter brandy bottles in the office trash. She tried to talk to him about it, but Sam shrugged her off and told her to get back to work.

Things became worse when Rico stopped by again, after hours at the office. Sam was drunk.

"We need another property," Rico said.

"I can't, Man. Do what you have to do to me, but I can't!"

"You don't have a choice. Otherwise, little Emily will disappear, never to be seen again. Poor Marigold will lose her only child." Rico slowly shook his head.

"No! Leave Emily out of this. It's my fault, not hers. Hurt me, not her."

"We can't hurt you. We need you. Plus, you'll get a bigger bonus."

"I don't want the money. I want this to be over." Sam began crying.

"I'll be back for the keys in one week."

Sam sank to the floor after Rico left. He didn't see any way out. He couldn't live knowing his stupidity might cost Emily her life. He thought of suicide more than once over the past months, and he brought a gun to work thinking he would be able to end things, but every time he tried, he couldn't pull the trigger.

He opened his desk drawer to reveal several bottles of Ibuprofen and bottles of booze he bought over the recent weeks. He opened a new liter of brandy and started taking handfuls of pills.

After he finished, he wrote a note to Anthony detailing what happened. At the end he added, *I'm sorry,* before he passed out at his desk.

Emily arrived the following morning and shook her head at finding the office door unlocked. She turned on the coffee pot and started her morning duties by emptying the trash bins. When she walked into Sam's office, she found him draped over his desk, unconscious and covered in vomit.

She immediately called 911, thinking he was drunk again, then she called Anthony and told him she quit. She walked into Sam's office again and noticed the empty pill bottles strewn across the floor.

She called 911 again and told them she believed it was a suicide attempt. The operator asked if she could feel Sam's pulse, then guided Emily through the process, because she didn't know how.

Emily felt nothing. The operator told her to stay on the phone, but Emily hung up and called Anthony again, crying hysterically.

Unable to understand her, Anthony ran to his car and drove to the Woodbridge office. En route, he called Alfonse and told him to meet him there.

Alfonse arrived only minutes after Anthony. The parking lot was filled with emergency vehicles. An ambulance had its rear doors open, with two fire trucks behind it. Alfonse and Anthony walked into the office, as two police cars arrived.

Emily cried hysterically, while two paramedics worked to save Sam. Alfonse noticed the paper with Sam's handwriting on it, which he quickly slipped into his pocket before the responding officers came in.

Both were surprised to see their chief at the scene and immediately saluted.

"He's a family member," Alfonse said. "Go ahead and do your jobs."

The paramedics loaded Sam into the ambulance. Anthony tried to console Emily and learn what happened. Alfonse spoke to the paramedics. Sam was still alive but in critical condition. They promised to do everything they could.

Anthony, leaving Emily with the police, got in his car with Alfonse in the passenger seat to follow the ambulance to the hospital. As they drove, Alfonse took out Sam's note and began reading it aloud. Both men were stunned by the contents.

The situation felt surreal to Anthony, but Alfonse had to face the reality that Sam accepted money to help a Hispanic gang. The men drove the rest of the journey in silence.

"Don't tell anyone about the letter yet," Alfonse cautioned. "We can discuss this once we've seen Sam."

Sam was in the trauma bay of the Level One Trauma Center. Looking through the door window, they saw medical staff working on Sam. One nurse stood on a stool to administer CPR. Another placed a tube in his mouth.

A nurse walked to the door and led Anthony and Alfonse to a small room adjacent to the ER. "Wait here. The doctor will want to talk to you."

They dutifully sat in silence until a female doctor in a white coat informed them Sam was still in critical condition but was stabilized.

"He'll be sent to the ICU for care," she said. "The next twenty-four hours will be critical. You should get some coffee and be ready to wait. We're giving him the best care we can."

Alfonse and Anthony went to the almost-empty cafeteria and sat at a corner table near a window. Breakfast was over, and the staff prepared for the lunch crowd.

"This isn't good for Sam," Alfonse said.

Anthony nodded as if in trance. "Do you think he'll make it?" he asked, his voice cracking.

"I pray to God he will, but then he faces serious legal problems."

"What do you mean?"

"He took money from those thugs to turn a blind eye. He also provided them another rental to sell drugs elsewhere."

Anthony became frightened. "You can't be serious. He had no choice."

"He had a choice, Anthony. My God, I'm the Chief of Police! He should've come to me, and we would've stopped all this. Now he faces serious prison time—if he survives." He put his head in his hands with his elbows propped on the table.

"No, Alfonse. We have to save him. He's been through hell and back. We can't turn our backs on him. He's family."

Alfonse stood and walked around the cafeteria before returning to the table.

"We have to get Sam out of here as soon as possible," Alfonse said. "We'll find a rehab facility somewhere out of state. No one knows about the drug gang yet, and, more importantly, the gang doesn't know what's happened.

"Let's get Emily out of the picture, too, with Marigold. Emily is already traumatized, so it won't be difficult. Perhaps we can offer them both a vacation. I'll leave that up to you.

"I'll have a task force raid both houses simultaneously and put these thugs in jail. At the least, I'll make life very difficult for them. I'll need your help with that, too. The less who are involved, the more chance we have of success."

"Whatever it takes, I'll do it."

"I need you to deliver a bag to each home sometime during the night."

"What's in the bags?"

"You don't need to know. It's better that you don't."

"Anthony!" someone called.

He turned to see his mother, father, and a few other close relatives walking into the cafeteria.

"I have to go," Alfonse said quietly. "I'll be in touch."

As Alfonse slipped away, Anthony explained what happened.

Alfonse returned to Police Headquarters to arrange for a SWAT team and police meeting at four o'clock. At shift change, he let himself into the basement evidence room and acquired four sawed-off shotguns without any identification marks. Placing them in a duffel bag, he took them to his office, then left.

The men's bathroom was immediately above the evidence room. Alfonse opened the door and set up a sign that read *Out of Order* just outside the door. Back inside, he turned on the hot and cold taps and plugged the sink with a rag he found before going back to his office.

Four hours later, he was advised there was a flood in the evidence room. The janitor must've left the tap running when he cleaned. All evidence was hurriedly removed from the evidence room to preserve it.

During the chaos, Alfonse took the duffel bag with the shotguns and placed them in his car. He set another duffle bag with two lists on them beside it. Some of the names had lines through them, some didn't. The mayor's name was on the list, along with Alfonse's name, the DA's name, and the name of a prominent judge.

He returned to the large squad room for his four o'clock meeting.

"We have gained information about two drug houses in the area," he began. "We believe the gang running both houses is planning an imminent hit on a courthouse judge. I have already contacted the courthouse, and all the judges are under FBI surveillance and protection."

He turned to the computer on the podium and projected images of the homes and their surrounding areas onto a whiteboard. "Our informant says there are women and children in both homes. We will raid them both at 5:30 in the morning to take them by surprise. There are at least four gang members in each house, and the gang is most likely armed. Due to the imminent danger, we have to move fast.

"Members of the SWAT team wearing civilian clothes will check out the area prior to the raid to familiarize themselves with the targets. We'll rendezvous at four-thirty tomorrow morning at City Hall Police Headquarters, when any new information will be shared."

After the meeting, Alfonse called Anthony, who was still at the hospital. "Meet me at your loft. How is Sam?"

"Unconscious but still breathing on his own. His chances of survival are rising, but there's no way to know if he suffered brain damage."

Alfonse, arriving at the loft, let himself in and placed the two duffel bags on the table.

"What's in those?" Anthony asked.

"I don't want you to know. Don't look in them for your own sake. Take these two bags to the two rental houses dealing drugs. There will be a raid on both of them at five-thirty in the morning. Try to set each bag near the back door of each house and hide them but not too well. We want them found during the raid.

"Wear a hoodie and dark jeans. Drop the bags around four o'clock. There shouldn't be anyone around then. If one of the houses has a dog, take some meat to make it quiet down. If you can't get a bag to the back door, plant it somewhere near the house."

It was a dark, cloudy, moonless night, so Anthony dropped the first bag off easily. His biggest fear was to encounter a dog. He was terrified of large dogs after being bitten as a child. He carried a large sirloin steak in a baggie just in case. He was lucky to find no one around and no dogs.

The second location was more complicated. There was no dog, but the gate was padlocked. He followed the chain-link fence around the house until it reached a tree. After tossing the bag over the fence, he shinnied up and dropped to the other side.

A car came by, so he hid beside the tree and waited until it passed the house. He set the bag near the back door and covered it with an old, dirty tarp laying in the backyard. Just as he tossed the tarp over the bag, a large, black snake fell out.

Anthony took one terrified look before bolting to the tree and vaulted over the fence using the tree for support. Somehow, he didn't scream. He didn't stop running until he reached his car two blocks away.

He was still shaking when he returned to his loft. After a stiff drink, he managed a couple hours of sleep, but his adrenalin level was too high for any real rest. Finally, he got up and showered.

At five o'clock at City Hall and Police Headquarters, the rooms buzzed with activity from members of the FBI, SWAT teams, police officers, DEA, ATF, and Social Services.

"We have new intelligence that advises us there are likely to be weapons in the homes," Alfonse told them.

All the participants wore Kevlar vests and sipped coffee from paper cups. After the briefing, the men left.

Carefully hidden watchers reported that both homes seemed quiet.

At five-thirty, all radios clicked, then someone shouted, "Go! Go! Go!"

The men breached the doors with battering rams. Within seconds, the houses were swarming with law enforcement. Children cried, as all rooms were searched, and the occupants were forced to lie down with their hands behind their backs.

Once the all clear was given at each home, social workers retrieved the children and took them away. The occupants were taken to the police station and placed under custody. Comprehensive searches of both homes began. Men checked the attic, the basements, and all the contents of drawers and cupboards. Mattresses were overturned and searched.

After sunrise, the surrounding yards were searched. An old shed at one home had to be searched, too.

The duffel bags were quickly found and opened. Within each bag were two sawed-off shotguns and lists of names.

Photographs of the weapons and lists were taken before the ATF secured and processed the weapons into evidence bags. They sealed the homes with yellow police tape, and two officers were stationed at each one to ensure no one breached the crime scene.

Back at headquarters, the lists were studied. It was clear the names with lines through them had been murdered or were reported missing. The others were assumed to be the next targets.

Judge Brown was on the list, a strict man who had no tolerance for drugs. He gave many gang members the maximum sentence. Chief Alfonse Paselli, the DA, and several prosecutors were also on the lists.

By the end of the day, charges for the gang ranged from possession of drugs, possession of illegal firearms, and intent to distribute and sell drugs within a school zone. The DA hoped

First-Degree Murder and Manslaughter could be added after further investigation. Each gang member appeared before a judge for arraignment. All were held without bond.

With the gang safely off the street, Alfonse joined Anthony at the hospital. He didn't mention the raid in front of the family and simply asked if anyone knew why Sam might wish to end his life.

"Maybe it was something involving a recent girlfriend," Anthony suggested.

Sam remained in a drug-induced coma while ICU doctors monitored his progress. His body fought to process the massive amount of Ibuprofen he ingested. At times, the doctors lowered his sedatives to see if he responded to commands.

They were encouraged when Sam was able to squeeze his hand and move his feet. His kidneys, however, were still not functioning.

As days passed, Sam was gradually taken off the ventilator and off the critical list. Although conscious, he was confused and became agitated at times. He was moved from ICU to a step-down unit but was too sick to go home.

The doctor recommended he be placed in a rehab facility, where others could monitor his care and move him toward independent living again. Anthony volunteered to find the best facility he could.

Fortunately, the best was the Tranquility Center in Florida, with an intensive inpatient program promoting positive medical and mental health while detoxifying from a drug overdose and alcohol consumption. The location was far enough away that Sam would be safe from retaliation from the Hispanic gang.

One week after Sam's overdose, he was on a medical flight to West Palm Beach, Florida. His condition improved, with his kidneys working at 80%. He still had periods of agitation, but those were improving slowly. His initial program was scheduled for two months. He did well in the program, but he still struggled with self-worth. He couldn't tell anyone why he took the overdose due to criminal repercussions, so his mental health recovery was slow.

Back in Minneola, Anthony's life slowly calmed down. Emily quit her job with a generous severance package from Anthony. He asked her not to discuss the incident, claiming it was a very private family matter. In her naïveté, she agreed. Emily and her mother, Marigold, accepted a vacation in the Caribbean, with Anthony driving them to the airport.

Another couple in Minneola were talking to anyone who would listen. They were evicted from the second rental to allow the drug dealers to operate and were still incensed. They contacted city officials, Social Services, and the local newspaper. Finally, the news reached Anthony, who immediately contacted the couple and explained Sam suffered a nervous breakdown and evicted the wrong people.

He immediately found them a newer, nicer home and reduced the rent by 50% for the first year. They were extremely happy, especially when Anthony promised to notify all the other agencies involved, including their bank and credit agencies, to put the record straight.

Unfortunately, some damage was done. The information about the eviction ended up on Special Agent Elizabeth McLeary's desk when she did a few background checks on the addresses of the raided drug homes in Minneola.

Six

After two weeks of living at the Park Hotel, Beth McCann couldn't wait to move into her new rental home. It was completely furnished, so she stored her personal items in a storage unit in Minneola. She rented the smallest U-Haul truck available and soon realized it wasn't big enough for all her boxes, bikes, kitchenware, and other things from the unit. She had to make two trips.

She drove to the rental home and began unpacking, knowing she faced a second run. The summer heat was thick with humidity, and she was already overheated from driving the truck, which had no air-conditioning. She pulled her red hair back into a ponytail, donned a baseball cap, and wore denim shorts with a white T-shirt. The shirt was filthy from lifting boxes, and she had a dirty smear down her left cheek.

She backed into the driveway, opened the tailgate, and began unpacking boxes through the propped-open front door of her new home to set them in the middle of the living room.

Although she marked all the boxes with the proper room names, she had only four hours to make two runs with the truck, so she had to stack everything as fast as she could. Jogging out the front door to get another box from the tailgate of the truck, she stopped just before running into a man who suddenly appeared.

"I'm so sorry!" She panted and stepped back. "I'm moving in, and I'm running out of time."

"You must be my new tenant. In fact, I believe we've met. I'm Joe Jackson. We met at the park when you had a slight problem with your shoe."

"Oh, God, was that you?" She blushed. "That dry-cleaning ticket of yours cost me a new pair of shoes."

"No, the ticket was for my friend, Anthony. I was the other one."

"Oh. Well, I'm Beth, your new tenant." She offered a dirty hand to shake, then pulled it back when she saw the dirt.

"Why are you running late?" Joe asked.

"I rented the smallest U-Haul only to find out it was too darn small. Now I have to make two trips, but I've only got the truck for four hours."

"Hold on." Joe walked down the path and into the next house. He called something, but Beth didn't catch it.

She continued emptying her truck. A box in her hands, she turned to find Joe with another man who resembled him.

"Then there were two," she said.

"Beth, this is Phil, my brother. We both live next door. We'll give you a hand."

"Are you sure?" She hoped they wouldn't change their minds.

"Yep. We'll knock this out in no time, then we'll follow you to the storage unit and help you at that end."

"Do you do this for all your new tenants?"

"Only the Irish ones," Phil said.

"Was it the red hair or the freckles that gave it away?" She laughed.

Emptying the first truck quickly, they had the second load delivered within two hours. The boxes went to their assigned rooms.

"I'd buy you both a drink, but as you can see, I'm hardly dressed for it." Beth collapsed on the sofa.

"No worries," Joe replied. "Why don't you settle in a bit and then come over for dinner around seven? It's just store-bought lasagna and red wine."

"Store-bought has never sounded so good. I can't remember when I last ate. I'll see you again at seven. Thanks again for all your help."

Over dinner, Beth explained she previously worked for the City Auditor in her previous town, but she had to give up the job when both her parents were diagnosed with Alzheimer's. Her father passed away first, leaving her mother totally dependent on Beth. As she described her mother's deterioration, her eyes filled with tears.

Her mother finally passed two months earlier. She sold her parents' home to pay their medical bills and needed a new start. She had enough money to get by for a couple months before she needed a job.

Phil and Joe explained their mother was from Ireland and was also diagnosed with Alzheimer's. They bought the home Beth was renting originally for their mother, providing her with round-the-clock care until her condition reached the point where she needed a nursing home. They placed her in a beautiful care facility thirty miles away. One of them visited her every day. They also employed a full-time caregiver to be with her in the home to ensure she got proper care.

Beth was extremely impressed. "I couldn't afford a private nursing home, so I kept my mother at home as long as possible until she needed inpatient care. Once that happened, I visited every day until she passed."

They explained their construction company and the fact that they were contractors for the city.

"Do you know anyone who might help me get a job in the City Auditor's office?" Beth asked.

"We grew up with Anthony Vito, the City Inspector," Joe said. "When you're ready, we can introduce you."

The following day, Beth drove to City Hall to change the address on her driver's license. It was the fastest process she ever knew at City Hall. In her old town, it would have taken half the afternoon.

As she left the office, she heard someone call, "Beth?"

She turned and blushed when she saw it was the man who lost his dry-cleaning ticket.

"What are you doing here?" Anthony asked.

"What are *you* doing here? I'm sorry, but I forgot your name."

"Wow. I really made quite a first impression." He laughed. "You can't remember my name? It's Anthony Vito, and I work here. Your turn."

"You're the City Inspector?"

"Yes, but you didn't answer my question."

"What was it again?"

"Why are you here?"

"Oh, to change the address on my driver's license."

"Are you living in town?

"Yes. I'm renting a place and will need a job soon. My landlords say they know you."

"Don't tell me you're Phil and Joe's new gal?"

"No, I'm their new renter." She smiled. "You know what they say, 'It's not what you know when you're looking for a job, it's who you know.'"

"I'm familiar with the concept."

"Well, I'm looking for a job with the City Auditor's office. I have experience. I was in my last job for six years."

"I happen to know the City Auditor really well. He's my cousin, Leo Catolina. The only thing is, he plays everything by the book, unlike me. Tell you what. We're having a Memorial Day picnic at the state park. Joe and Phil will be there, along with my family. Come with them, and I'll introduce you."

"Are you sure?"

"It's the least I can do for breaking your shoe."

"Very funny, but I would be very grateful."

"It's settled. Come ready to play football. It's a family tradition at the Memorial Day picnic."

"Be careful. I happen to be an excellent and extremely competitive football player. You may need me on your team."

"Done. Got to go—see you at the picnic."

The following day, Beth returned to the Melville FBI Satellite Office in Suffolk County to update her team. She took the train and told the Jackson boys she was returning to her former home to finalize some of her parents' affairs.

At the office, she briefed the team about meeting the owners of Jackson Construction and Anthony Vito, the City Inspector.

"Anthony is also related to Leo Catolina, the City Auditor," she added.

On the wall, she and her team created a large board with photos and a family tree. At the top was Minneola Chief of Police Alfonse Paselli. Directly under him, Beth added a line with photos of Anthony Vito and Leo Catolina, along with a photo of Sam Garillo from Woodbridge Rentals. Beth wasn't sure if Garillo was related to Vito and Catolina.

Under Anthony's photo, she added photos of Phil and Joe Jackson, Vito's preferred contractors. Farther across the board were pictures of Carlos and Andreas Martinez and Cousin Miguel Martinez. Those still had to be linked to the investigation.

"I've been invited to a family picnic by Vito and will attend with Joe and Phil Jackson," she said. "I hope to meet more of the family, which will help the investigation."

Memorial Day was a glorious day in Minneola. Temperatures were in the mid-seventies, the sun shone, and it was perfect for a football game. Anthony reserved the pavilion at the state park and had it decorated with red, white, and blue streamers and balloons. A Bounce Castle was set up for the kids, and a large smoker gave off incredible smells of cooking meat. A DJ worked from the back of the pavilion playing Beach Boys hits. An ice-cream truck was parked on the grass, and someone set up a station for face painting.

Beside the ice-cream truck was a bar that served only soft drinks, because alcohol was illegal in the park. When Beth went for a drink, however, she realized the alcohol was just under the table and asked for a beer. She received her drink in a red plastic cup with a top.

At least one hundred people filled the pavilion drinking, eating, and having a great time. Seeing Anthony, she waved when he looked her way. He immediately worked his way through the crowd to hug her. His pleasure was clear.

"Where are the guys?" he asked.

"They went to the nursing home to pick up their mom. They'll bring her to the party for a bit."

"Great. I haven't seen her in ages. Come on. Let me introduce you to everyone." Taking her hand, he pulled her to a large table in the middle of the pavilion.

"Hey, everyone! This is Beth. She's renting next door to the Jacksons."

They smiled warmly at her.

"Beth, here we go. Listen carefully, because there will be a test," Anthony said. "This is my mom, Maria. That handsome fellow over there is my father, Anthony, Senior. This is my cousin, Leo Catolina and his wife, Maria. Their kids are in the Bounce Castle. This is my other cousin, Maria Pasquale.

"This is cousin Angelo and his wife, Mia. Sitting beside them is my cousin Alfonse Paselli and his wife, Margaret. Then we have Angelo and Donna. I won't try to tell you which kids belong to who, but these are Michael, Maria, Emilia, Patrizio, Caprice, Maria, and Bellisa. The rest of the kids are here somewhere."

"Holy moly, you have a large family!" Beth exclaimed.

"Yep, and not all of them are here."

"How many more are there?"

"My cousin Stephano and his wife, Antonia, are on vacation, and my other cousin, Sam, isn't well right now."

"Aw, that's a shame. Will Sam be OK?"

"Yes. He's out of town getting treatment. We're very close, and I miss him."

Before she could answer, he pulled her to another table.

"Beth, this is my ex-wife Daniella and my twin boys, Mario and Matteo. Daniella, this is Beth. She's renting next to the Jacksons."

Daniella stood and shook Beth's hand. "Don't you love Joe and Phil?" She didn't wait for an answer and continued, "If I hadn't married this loser—just kidding, Anthony—I wouldn't have been able to choose Phil or Joe." She hugged Anthony and smiled fondly at him. "Are you dating either of them?" she asked Beth.

"Oh, no. We're just friends." She tried to recover from such a blunt question. "I don't believe in mixing relationships and business."

"I like her." Daniella turned away from Anthony and shouted at Matteo, who tried to poke Mario in the eye.

"Never a dull moment," Anthony said, as they walked away.

"You certainly have a good relationship, considering you're divorced."

"I didn't like her for a while, but we've been friends since we were kids. She's my kids' mother and a good one. We do well as friends but badly as a married couple."

"Amazing." Turning, she saw Joe and Phil pushing their mother in a wheelchair.

"Maria, you look fantastic!" Anthony shouted, walking toward them.

Oh, Lord, another Maria, Beth thought.

"Let me take you over to Mom and Dad," Anthony said loudly over the Beach Boys music.

"Santa Maria, it's Maria!" Anthony's mother shouted. "Anthony, come see Maria."

Beth was completely confused. While everyone said hello, she walked to Phil and Joe and asked if she could get them a drink. As the trio walked toward the bar, they argued over who would be the designated driver for their mother later.

"I'll do it," Beth said. "I had only one sip of this beer, and I'm not that keen. Plus, I owe you one."

The Jackson brothers didn't need any more persuading. They ordered beer, then they walked to the smoker and piled their plates high with ribs, pulled pork, and beans. Finding an empty table in the pavilion, they began eating. A moment later, Anthony bounced over and plunked down beside Beth.

"Which one of your cousins is the County Auditor?" she asked.

"The one in the white shirt. That's Leo and his wife, Maria. He's sitting beside my other cousin, Maria Pasquale, the DA."

"Geez. Does everyone in your family work for City Hall?"

Anthony thought for a minute.

"Sam doesn't," Phil said.

"The one who's sick?"

"Yeah, but he's getting better. Come on, Beth. Let's bounce in the castle."

She protested, but he took her hands and led her away.

By the time she crawled out of the castle, Beth was red in the face. She grabbed a Diet Coke and sat on the grass, panting.

"Rest up," Joe said. "Football's next."

"Jesus, is this how you guys relax?"

"Are you chickening out? I heard you're quite a player."

"Absolutely not. Just give me a minute to rest." She lay back on the grass.

On the way back from driving the older woman to the nursing home, Beth asked the brothers what was wrong with Sam, adding that Anthony talked passionately about him.

"You need to ask Anthony," Joe said. "He's very sensitive on that subject. He's being treated at a facility in West Palm Beach."

She dropped the subject and teased the brothers about how she scored the winning touchdown against them.

Seven

Beth handed in her application at the Personnel Office at City Hall. As Anthony instructed her, she added his name as one of her references. Anthony also spoke to Leo about her, who simply said, "She'll have the same chance as all the rest."

Beth was called in for an interview with Leo and the Personnel Manager, Kathy Walker. The interview went well, as Beth described her previous duties in the Auditor's Department at her hometown. The computer system in Minneola was the same one she used before. She felt she connected well with Leo and Kathy. Kathy told Beth they would check her references and let her know.

Back at the Melville FBI Office, Beth's team located Sam Garillo at the Tranquility Center in West Palm Beach. After a brief investigation, they found Sam overdosed at the Woodbridge Rental Office around the same time as the raids on the two drug homes.

After a week in intensive care at a local trauma center, Sam was transferred to the rehab facility. The 911 call came from Emily Winters, who told the operator she was the Office Manager who worked with Sam.

The line on the board with Sam's photo was joined to the photos of Anthony Vito and Alfonse Paselli. Another photo was added for Maria Pasquale, the DA. Beth's team located Emily living with her mother, Marigold, and working part-time in the high school's administration office. Another team planned to go undercover to investigate Emily's role in Sam's overdose.

The team also needed to examine the police records from the drug raids at the Woodbridge Rental homes. Normally, that was done in conjunction with the DA's office, but since the DA was related to the Chief of Police, and the case was ongoing, the files couldn't be removed from the Minneola Police Department.

With the DEA also involved in the case, a team of Melville FBI agents were detailed to the DEA. Securing a conference room at the police department, they worked on many boxes of files related to the case. They were eager not to alert the Chief of Police that they were also checking what part he played in the investigation. To cover their tracks, they made sure to praise him for a job well done.

Beth was hired for the new job and began working in the City Auditor's office the following week. She soon picked up the way they did things and quickly made herself an integral part of the team. She saw Anthony frequently, and they ate lunch together in the park where they first met about three times a week. She made excuses to work late at night in the office to peruse the records, including complaints and recommendations.

Susan Mitchell, the Special Agent investigating Emily, went undercover as an Agency temp worker assigned to the administration office where Emily worked. Emily was annoyed that a temp was hired, because she requested a full-time position. Emily was a sweet young woman, and she soon embraced Susan as a friend. They spent time together after work.

Susan rented an apartment near the school and invited Emily over for dinner one evening. Emily still lived with her mother and was impressed with Susan's apartment. On the fridge was a photo of a handsome young man.

"He's good-looking," Emily commented.

"That's my brother who recently passed away." With tears in her eyes, she told Emily he was a talented, spirited young man who dated a girl who used cocaine.

"He was hooked the first time he tried it. Within a week, he was dead, overdosed on bad cocaine mixed with Fentanyl. I found him in his apartment. The scene won't leave my mind."

Emily put her arm around Susan's shoulders and said, "I witnessed something similar, and I'll never forget it, either."

"Was it a family member?"

Emily hesitated, then explained how she found her boss overdosed at the office. "He survived, but he's no longer in town. I quit my job, because I couldn't face going back there."

"My brother's name was Mark. Who was your boss?"

"Sam Garillo."

As the evening progressed, and a second bottle of wine was opened, Emily told Susan all about Woodbridge Rentals and Rico. the tattooed Hispanic who made a pass at her.

"Mr. Vito took care of me financially after I said I wanted to quit," Emily added.

"Who's he?"

"Anthony Vito. He works at City Hall and owns Woodbridge Rentals."

"He sounds like a great boss."

Susan returned to the Melville FBI office to report her finding that Anthony was the owner of the anonymous trust that ran Woodbridge Rentals. She confirmed Sam was Anthony's cousin who overdosed the day before the rental homes were raided.

Her next job was to find out who Rico, the tattooed Hispanic who had the hots for Emily, was. She needed to know why Sam evicted the previous owners of one of the rental homes, too.

The FBI agent who was detailed to the DEA combed through the police files from the rental home drug raids. All the files were in order, with no red flags. An informant alerted the Chief of Police about drugs being sold from the rental homes. He also told the Chief that the gang was targeting a senior judge who had recently incarcerated several drug dealers, which explained the Chief's quick reaction to launch the raid.

The only missing piece of information was the informant's name, but that wasn't unusual. Many high-level informants had their names hidden. Since the informant had access to the Chief of Police, though, the team assumed he was a high-level person.

Beth, who had been undercover many times, began to feel uncomfortable around Anthony Vito. In the past, her undercover work had her dating suspects, and it never bothered her. It was part of her job, a means to an end. She walked away from those cases and the people she met without any regrets.

That time was different. She liked Anthony and admired his family loyalty. He watched over his parents, aunts, uncles, and cousins religiously. He was involved with their concerns and problems, and he worked hard to keep everyone happy. Most amazing was his relationship with his ex-wife, Daniella, and his children. He was a doting father, and she was his best friend. Decisions about the children were made together, and he often dropped in after work to have dinner with them.

He spoke freely about his family to Beth over lunch, often voicing concerns about someone's health. One lunchtime in the park, he chatted about his Aunt Maria. Without warning, he asked Beth to have dinner with him. Every cell in her body told her to refuse and keep the relationship platonic. Unfortunately, she heard herself accepting.

Dressing for dinner was a big challenge for Beth that night. Nothing she tried on felt right. She settled for a tight-fitting black dress, black high heels, and an elegant string of pearls. After twisting her hair up into a clasp, she looked into the mirror and smiled, then she waited for him to pick her up.

Anthony was visibly taken aback at her appearance, and she blushed when he said how gorgeous she looked. Considering they ate lunch together often, she had a hard time conversing with him that night, perhaps due to how stunning he looked, too. He wore a sharp black suit, red tie, cufflinks, and polished black shoes.

The two of them made heads turn when they walked into the restaurant. Anthony chose an Italian restaurant owned by a relative. Although it was warm outside, there was a crackling fire in the old-fashioned fireplace. Beth was delighted when their table was beside the fire.

The lights were low, with flickering candles on each table. It was possibly the most-elegant restaurant she ever dined in. The food was delicious, and she let him order for her, because he knew all the dishes. He also ordered a bottle of Italian red wine.

As the wine flowed, Beth's difficulty with conversation disappeared. They chatted as if they'd known each other all their lives. When dessert arrived, so did a violinist, who serenaded them. Beth felt totally relaxed sitting with Anthony until he stood, took her hand, and guided her to a small space between tables. He gently pulled her toward him and began dancing, much to the delight of the patrons and the violinist. A round of applause followed their dance when they returned to their table. Beth was radiant, her cheeks flushed from the wine and the impromptu dance.

A taxi took them to Beth's apartment. She couldn't invite him in, because she had work files waiting on the dining room table. Anthony told the driver to wait, then he walked her to her front door, where he gave her a hug, a kiss on the cheek, and whispered, "We must do this more often."

Beth's heart raced, as he walked back to the taxi, and she entered her apartment.

The following evening, she worked late at the office to go over several files she needed to study. The first file didn't have anything interesting, but the second contained information she needed. It was titled *RESCUE—Origination and Implementation.*

She learned that RESCUE was a new program implemented in Minneola two years earlier. The acronym stood for Residents Emergency Services Caring for the Underprivileged Elderly. The mayor implemented the program during his previous constituency, and it proved very successful.

She learned the program specifically addressed emergencies and code violations that posed threats to the health and safety of the elderly, affecting the live-ability of their home. The assistance, paid by the city, was targeted to enable seniors to continue living independently in their own homes. The program was run through the City Inspector's office. Applications were sent to City Inspector Anthony Vito, who visited the homes to determine if they met the criteria, then an independent, licensed contractor was scheduled to do the work. Once the work was completed, Anthony inspected it. If satisfied, he filed approval for City Hall to pay the contractors.

In the file, she found several complaints for people who were approved for the program yet had to wait for months for jobs to be completed. After one complaint, on which the mayor wrote

Unacceptable, there were no more. Beth assumed procedures were put into place to resolve the backlog.

Then she found the RESCUE files of all jobs completed since implementation of the program, listed by date. As she thumbed through them, she realized all the work was done by Jackson Construction, Joe and Phil's company. That was a surprise. She assumed Jackson Construction was only a small operation. When Phil described it to her, he said the most-difficult part of running the company was finding decent workers. They had four good construction workers who took orders from Joe, as well as an office administration clerk, while Phil did the rest of the administration himself. He added they never had to market the company, because they always had work.

She pulled a few dates from the file. On the first, six jobs were completed. The following day, eight were completed. As she went through the files and scope of work, it became obvious there was no way a small company could have completed all those jobs in one day. She tried to find information that would indicate Jackson subcontracted some of the jobs without success. She made photocopies of some of the larger completed jobs before putting the files away.

Over the weekend, she spent more time than usual with Phil and Joe.

"How's business going?" she asked casually.

"Really busy," they said.

"I have a friend from my hometown who's an incredible construction worker with his own business. If you ever get too busy and need help, I'm sure I could get him to subcontract for you."

"We tried subcontracting a few years ago," Joe said. "We always got burned. If we do it ourselves, we know it'll be done professionally and correctly."

Sunday evening, she cooked dinner for all her "boys," as she called them. Anthony, Joe, and Phil sat at her small dining room table enjoying a Sunday roast with all the trimmings. After dinner, they relaxed at Joe and Phil's house and drank liquor from their cabinet.

The three men smoked cigars and drank brandy, while Beth enjoyed a glass of Bailey's. Finally, she said, "I have to go back home to attack the dirty dishes."

Anthony stood up with her. "I'll help."

At her house, they quickly established a system with Beth rinsing and Anthony placing items in the dishwasher. It was almost eleven o'clock by the time they finished.

Beth groaned, knowing she had to get up early for work. Anthony took that as his cue to leave. He grabbed his car keys and pulled her into a hug.

It seemed to last forever. Beth looked up at him, as he looked down, and their mouths met. Anthony kissed her gently. When he kissed her a second time, she felt as if she were floating.

"I think I'm falling in love with you," he whispered.

Beth smiled, took his hand, and led him to her bedroom.

The following morning, Anthony dropped Beth a block away from the office, so she could walk into City Hall herself. Although exhausted, she managed to complete her work with a constant smile on her face.

"Do you know you're grinning like the Cheshire Cat?" Leo asked.

Unable to keep her eyes open, she didn't work late that night. She caught a ride home with a coworker, crawled into her unmade bed, wrinkled from the night of passion she shared with Anthony, and closed her eyes to remember that evening.

Her ringing cell phone interrupted her reverie. It was her boss, Assistant Special Agent in Charge Tony Kuertz, from the FBI office in Melville. Sitting upright in bed, she tried to concentrate on what he told her.

"I need you to return to Melville in the morning so all the team can update each other with their findings."

"I need to arrange time off from the City Auditor's office."

"Deal with it. Be there by ten at the latest."

Eight

Beth called Anthony from the train. "One of my aunts has been in an accident. I'm her emergency contact. She's in the hospital."

"You should've let me take you."

"I don't know how long I'll be staying."

"Please stay in touch."

At the FBI office, the conference room was filled with team members working on the rental home drug case. The chart with all the photographs hung on the wall. Anthony's photo had lines connecting it to everyone except the Martinez gang.

The team detailed to the DEA, who inspected the files at the Police Department, spoke first.

"The Chief of Police acted appropriately due to a possible threat to other civil servants in Minneola. The only thing we couldn't determine was the name of the informant who called him. We checked with Chief Paselli about this, and he refused to disclose the name.

"We found there was an incident at police headquarters the day prior to the raid. A flood in the men's bathroom seeped through the floor and went into the evidence room directly below. They lost a large amount of evidence, as well as the ceiling and walls of the evidence room. They had to remove the remaining evidence to another area until the room was restored.

"We asked to see the roster of evidence stored in the room to ensure no weapons were removed, but, due to the overwhelming amount of items they took from the room, no one could assure us that everything on the roster was still there. Once the flood was discovered, they photographed everything that was removed. We went through those photos, and nothing even closely resembled the guns seized from the rental homes during the raid."

The next report came from Special Agent Susan Mitchell, who befriended Emily Winters. "Her boss at Woodbridge Rentals was Sam Garillo. On the day before the raid, Sam took an overdose at the office, and Emily found him unconscious when she came in for work in the morning. We know Sam is Anthony Vito's cousin, but we discovered that Anthony is also the owner of the anonymous trust that owns Woodbridge.

"Sam is still an inpatient at the Tranquility Center in West Palm Beach, Florida. Emily also told us about a Hispanic man, possibly Mexican, named Rico, who visited the Woodbridge Rental office several times. I haven't been able to locate him."

It was Beth's turn to update the team. "I found a city program called RESCUE, which was established by the Minneola mayor two years earlier. It involves the city paying for repairs to the homes of the elderly in Minneola so they can remain in their homes safely. Only one construction company does the work, Jackson Construction. In my estimation, there's no way such a small company could have completed all the work I found documented. I'm still investigating how the work was done."

After all members presented their findings, the focus for the next stage of the investigation had Beth continuing to look into the RESCUE program. Another team member would go undercover to interview Sam Garillo, while someone else would follow up with the family who was evicted from their Woodbridge home before it became a drug house. An agent was assigned to question the Martinez gang about the man called Rico Emily mentioned. The DEA team confirmed the weapons weren't taken from the police evidence room, so further investigations had to be made to determine the source of the weapons.

Beth returned to Minneola on the last train and was back in her apartment by seven o'clock. En route, she called the Auditor's Office and told them she'd be at work the following day and would stay late to catch up on work. She also called Anthony to advise him the same thing, then she dissuaded him from coming to her apartment, because she was still tired and upset from her aunt's accident.

Beth couldn't sleep. She never put herself in such a situation before. The number-one rule of undercover work was not to become emotionally attached to anyone under surveillance. She knew she was falling in love with Anthony and felt very close to Joe and Phil. Although she didn't understand how they were operating their business, her gut told her something was wrong.

Alfonse Paselli was a great guy but also the Chief of Police. There was no evidence of any wrongdoing, but her gut told her the same thing. How could she continue to pursue them as suspects? She couldn't tell Anthony the real reason she was in town, because too many people were involved.

She had to keep going with her investigation and find out what was going on, so she could decide how to move forward.

Beth met Anthony for a quick lunch the following day, explaining she was crazy busy at work and trying to catch up, so she would be working late that night.

"My aunt climbed a small ladder in her garage and then fell, giving her a head injury," she explained. "She's in the hospital but will be transferred to a rehab facility soon."

To change the subject, she asked, "How's your cousin, Sam, doing?"

"I'm picking him up from the facility in Florida and bringing him home this weekend. Would you like to come with me? I warn you it'll be a twenty-four-hour drive."

"I'd love to." She felt it would be advantageous to meet Sam.

Beth told the team Sam would be discharged on the coming weekend, and an undercover agent was immediately dispatched to interview him. Special Agent Bob Bond became Dr. Robert More, an exit counselor for Tranquility Rehabilitation who was introduced to Sam.

"When a patient leaves our facility," Dr. More said, "a doctor conducts an exit interview to ensure he's ready to leave and to establish plans for his future."

Sam, feeling excited about leaving, was very upbeat during the interview. "The treatment I received was great. I'd like to go back to my old job at Woodbridge Rentals."

"You've told other counselors that your job drove you to take an overdose. What will be different this time?"

"It'll be different, because the players have changed."

"What do you mean?"

Sam hesitated. "Well, I was under pressure from former renters to overlook certain behaviors. Now those renters are gone."

Playing devil's advocate, Dr. More asked, "What will you do if they come back?"

"They won't. After my therapy, I know how to handle myself better. My cousin's the Chief of Police, and another cousin owns the rental company. If anything happens again, I'll get them involved."

"Why are you so sure they won't come back?"

Sam squirmed in his chair. "They won't."

"Why not?"

Sam just shrugged. "They're in prison."

"Were they involved in illegal activity? Was that what made you clinically depressed?"

Sam nodded.

"Did you ever feel your life was at risk?"

Sam bowed his head. "Not only my life, but my secretary's."

"Do your cousins know about this, so they can protect you from anything like it in the future?"

Sam sighed. "Without them, I wouldn't be alive."

Dr. More nodded. "I'll clear you for departure from the clinic, and I'll advise your medical doctors about this conversation."

Special Agent Bob Bond wrote up the interview and presented it to the Melville team, with Beth joining via teleconference. Bob's information linked Anthony Vito and Chief Alfonse Paselli to the drug dealers, and it confirmed Paselli knew about the drug houses prior to the raid. That made it feasible that he could have planted the weapons at the drug homes.

Their initial investigations determined that the chief hadn't taken the weapons from the evidence room during the flood. According to the evidence room logs, he hadn't visited the room in six months before the flood.

"Are there any cameras near the evidence room?" someone asked.

No one knew. The team detailed to the DEA would return to the Minneola City Hall to investigate.

Special Agent Susan Mitchell needed to establish if Emily's crush, the man named Rico, was part of the drug gang. They needed to bring him in for questioning to substantiate Sam's story. Special Agent Bob Bond would contact the evicted couple who caused the fuss at City Hall to determine if they were evicted to allow the gang to operate another drug house. He also needed to locate the original eviction notice and see who signed it.

Special Agent Elizabeth McCleary would remain undercover as Beth McCann to establish what Anthony knew. She also had to determine how Jackson Construction and the City Inspector's office managed to complete the hundreds of RESCUE cases with only four workmen.

Beth secured copies from the RESCUE completion files. She tried to find obvious repairs, like roof replacements and work completed on the exterior of a home, so she could see the work herself.

After her first day back at the City Auditor's office, she drove to the first location on Crescent Drive to look at the new roof. She found the home, with an elderly woman sitting on the front porch.

Beth waved and walked toward her. "I'm from City Hall to check on the work that was done for you by the city."

"You must be mistaken," Ms. Johnson said. "I didn't have any roof work done."

Beth looked puzzled. "Did you apply for work to be done through the RESCUE program?"

"My neighbor filled out the application, but the city denied it. I still have buckets strategically placed inside. When it rains, I'll be ready."

"Thank you." Beth, returning to her car, drove to the second location, where part of a chain-link fence had fallen down during a storm. It was clear no work had been done.

She went from house to house and only once found that the work had been completed as stated in the documents.

The following day, Beth checked the payment paperwork on the homes. Each one had Anthony's signature stating he checked the work, and it met code. The next paper in the file was a copy of the check issued to Jackson Construction.

As she looked through various files, she came across the address for her own rental. After more digging, she found that work under the RESCUE program totaled $20,000 and was payable to Jackson Construction. It was for a new work that Beth knew had been done.

After the work was finished, the elderly lady who owned the home passed away, and it became abandoned. The home was sold to Woodbridge Rentals for $20,000—the same amount that was paid to repair the roof.

She followed the paperwork trail through the real-estate tax records and saw the home was sold again to Jackson Construction for $20,000. After a year, presumably when Mrs. Jackson lived there, the home was rented to a couple who qualified for Section 8 housing, and there was a record of payments made by the Section 8 office to Jackson Construction. Those payments stopped one month before Beth moved in.

She began checking the other RESCUE home that had been abandoned and found all were purchased by the anonymous trust that owned Woodbridge Rentals. Each became Section 8 housing, with payments routed to the Woodbridge office.

It was clear how Jackson Construction was able to complete all the RESCUE work. They didn't do it but still collected the money. Anthony not only falsified the inspection letters hoping to trigger the payments to Jackson Construction, he then bought the homes at undervalued prices before renting them out as Section 8 Affordable Housing, receiving guaranteed money from the city.

Beth felt sick. All she felt for Anthony at that moment was disgust. He was taking advantage of the city's elderly to line his own pockets. She thought of Ms. Johnson with buckets placed to catch leaks from her roof. Joe and Phil were just as bad, also taking advantage of the elderly. How could they do such a thing when their own mother was an elderly woman in need?

Beth decided she couldn't go to Florida with Anthony. She wouldn't be able to stand being around him that long. She called him later and said, "My aunt's being moved to a rehab facility, and I need to be there."

Anthony was already upset they hadn't spent as much time together during the week due to Beth's work schedule, and he became more frustrated not having her with him on the trip to get Sam. The whole point of driving to Florida was to spend time with her.

Anthony booked a flight to West Palm Beach on Saturday and rented a vehicle to pick up Sam. They would fly back together the same day.

After securing the tickets, Anthony decided to visit Beth unexpectedly. Her car was in the driveway, so she had to be home. He knocked and waited a long time for her to answer the door.

Beth frantically gathered her paperwork and shoved it into a cabinet, then she stripped off her clothes and ran the shower for a couple seconds before donning a toweling robe before answering.

"Hi," she said. "I was in the shower."

Anthony gently pulled her close. When she resisted, he knew something was wrong. "What's happening?"

"I'm worried about my aunt. The trauma to her head is worse than expected. She's been moved to ICU and won't be able to go to the rehab facility after all. I have to go see her right after I get off work Friday. I'll take the train to West Chester to reach the hospital."

Anthony sat on the sofa. "I'm so sorry. Can I take you instead of making you go by train? I booked airline tickets for the trip to Florida."

Shocked at how quickly he changed his plans, she said, "I already bought my train ticket. It'll be faster than by car."

He nodded. "Is anything else bothering you?"

"My head's spinning. I moved here to begin a new life, but my old life keeps calling me back. I wonder if I was being selfish by moving away."

"You can't go back to West Chester. You should stay here in Minneola with me."

She shook her head. "I'm not sure of anything right now. Too many things have come up. I need to spend time with my aunt to see just where I ought to live."

Anthony was visibly upset. "All right. I'll give you the space you need." He hugged her before he left. "Keep in touch."

She nodded.

Gently kissing her cheek, he left.

Nine

Beth took the train to Melville Friday after work and was ready to report to the rest of the team Saturday morning in the conference room.

Special Agent Susan Mitchell went first. "I spent time with Emily and discovered she knew nothing about any threat to her life. I also located Rico, who has an outstanding drug warrant. He's in Minneola, but I didn't want to alert the police, so I went down there with some of the team and brought him to our office here.

"At first, he denied any knowledge about Woodbridge until I mentioned Sam and Emily. I managed to convince him to talk to get a reduced sentence with the DA, especially after I told him the rest of the gang was in jail, they claimed the weapons were deliberately planted, and the Minneola DA refused to investigate. He saw it as an opportunity to rise within the gang by helping reduce their potential sentences.

"After that, he almost wouldn't shut up. He told me about his visits with Sam, his conversation with Emily, and about Marigold, Emily's mother. He even boasted about his favorite brass knuckles.

"When I broached the subject of weapons at the drug houses, he was adamant that they must've been planted. He admitted he carried a pistol, but the gang never owned any sawed-off shotguns. He substantiated everything Sam told Dr. More."

The team detailed to check out the Chief of Police were instructed to revisit City Hall and check the cameras near the evidence room. To reach that room, a person had to pass the emergency exit, so the cameras would catch anyone going down that hall.

After many hours of boring video tape, they saw the Chief of Police go down the hall five hours before the flood. He emerged from the room with large duffel bags. An inspection of the bags found at the raids showed they matched the bags in the Chief's hands.

Footage from the front door cameras showed the Chief setting the bags in his personal vehicle the same afternoon. By accessing traffic cameras, they followed him to the area of Anthony Vito's loft. Twenty minutes later, he was seen on the same camera going the opposite direction.

After dark, Anthony Vito's car was picked up by traffic cameras near the two rental homes. A gas station in the neighborhood also showed Anthony Vito's car parked near one of the rental homes, and he left the vehicle carrying a duffel bag. When he returned ten minutes later, he didn't have the bag.

They had enough evidence to substantiate the Chief of Police's involvement with planting weapons at the rental homes prior to the raids. There was also enough evidence to show he transported the weapons to Anthony, who placed the bags at the scene of the raids.

Special Agent Bob Bond spoke next. "The couple evicted from their rental home had to move out the week the drug dealers moved in. They complained to everyone, including City Hall, the police, and Social Services. They told me they were about to give up when Anthony Vito approached them and said Sam evicted the wrong couple. To compensate them for their trouble, Mr. Vito gave them a better rental and cut the rent by fifty percent. He also contacted the bank and their credit agencies to correct the mistake. The couple was very impressed with him."

It was Beth's turn. "It appears from my research that Anthony, Phil, and Joe concocted an elaborate scheme to steal money from City Hall. They did it by exploiting the city's elderly."

On the whiteboard, she displayed the paper trails showing how RESCUE applications were denied to homeowners but approved by City Inspector Anthony Vito.

"Anthony Vito and Jackson Construction submitted paperwork to the City Inspector stating the work was completed. Then Vito signed off on the paperwork to show the work met code. City Hall then paid Jackson Construction.

An investigation at the banking institutes used by Woodbridge Rentals and Jackson Construction shows that the funds from their fraudulent activities were split, with equal portions to Anthony, Joe, and Phil.

Anthony Vito also purchased a number of homes where RESCUE work was completed. It appears he researched which elderly homeowners were the least likely to have family claims to the homes once the homeowner died. He undervalued the abandoned homes and bought them through Woodbridge's anonymous trust and passed them to Woodbridge Rentals. Then the homes were rented to Section 8 families. With rent paid by the city, they were guaranteed timely payments.

Evidence supports Joe and Phil's participation in the scam. However, there is no evidence linking them to the drug homes, the subsequent police raids, or the planted weapons. I also determined there is no evidence linking Chief Paselli to the RESCUE scam.

Based on all this, the initial charges for Phil, Joe, and Anthony include corruption, embezzlement, fraud, money laundering, and tax evasion. Anthony will also face criminal aiding and abetting. Sam Garillo will face charges of criminal aiding and abetting, permitting drug abuse and corruption. Chief Paselli faces charges of corruption, violation of civil rights, criminal aiding and abetting, wrongful arrest, and imprisonment."

Elizabeth McLeary contacted the Suffolk District Court Judge J. Terry at his home and spent an hour explaining the case before requesting arrest warrants for Anthony Vito, Alfonse Paselli, Samuel Garillo, Philip Jackson, and Joseph Jackson. She also requested their personal and business accounts be frozen.

Judge Terry agreed with the charges and advised her the warrants would be available Monday morning. His Administrative Assistant, Janice Sorrento, would be in touch for the details.

She returned to her apartment in Melville on Saturday evening to find a voice message from Anthony.

"I'm about to board a flight back home to Long Island with Sam. Please get in touch."

She texted him a message that she was still at the hospital with her aunt and would call him Sunday. She then called Leo Catolina at home and told him she wouldn't be able to come on Monday, as she needed to make arrangements for her aunt who was still in ICU. He gave her as much time as she needed.

Elizabeth almost felt sorry for him, knowing the bombshell that would soon hit his family.

Janice Sorrento was a distant relative of Anthony Vito. She was scheduled to work at the Suffolk County Courthouse on Sunday to issue any warrants received Friday night and Saturday. She didn't like attending Mass on Saturday nights, but that was her only option when she worked weekends.

After Mass, Janice and her husband met another couple and spent the evening at a small Italian restaurant in Melville. During the evening, Janice noticed an attractive young woman with red hair pulled back into a ponytail come into the restaurant. She seemed familiar, but Janice couldn't place her. Her husband asked her a question, and she forgot about it.

Sunday morning was a miserable day, with heavy rain and gray skies. Janice unlocked her office door, dropped her purse on her desk, and hung her wet coat on a coat stand in the corner. She filled the coffee pot with water and set it to *Brew*. The aroma quickly filled the air, as she turned on the old radio on her windowsill to a classical music channel. Once again, coffee and music would get her through the day.

Her Inbox was filled to overflowing. She flicked through the papers and thought she saw the name Vito. Picking up the pile, she searched until she found it, only to discover it was one of ten pages.

She sat down to read the paperwork and was stunned by what she found. She was about to prepare warrants for her cousins Anthony, Sam, and Alfonse, along with the Jackson brothers, who she also knew well. Her heart raced, and she felt sick to her stomach.

Unable to decide what to do, she lifted the telephone receiver to call her husband, then hung up. Every time she thought of who to share the news with, she realized she couldn't. She sat at her desk, elbows on the surface and her head in her hands, and suddenly remembered the woman at the restaurant.

She'd seen the same woman with Anthony at the family picnic!

She grabbed the first page of the paperwork and saw the contact person was an FBI agent named Elizabeth McLeary, but the woman at the party was introduced as Beth. A quick computer search gave her the name of Special Agent Elizabeth McLeary, and the photo that came up was definitely Beth.

"Damn it!" It was clear Anthony and the entire family were under FBI surveillance. She grabbed her coat and purse, locked the office door, and ran to her car. There was a pay phone at the bus station.

She called Anthony from the pay phone and quickly filled him in, making him gasp.

"I can stall the warrant until Monday late afternoon or evening, but you need to tell everyone who's involved in this. If you ever tell anyone about this call, I'll lose my job and will probably face criminal charges. Your new sweetheart is an undercover FBI agent. Don't reveal your source to anyone. I could go to jail over this."

Anthony didn't reply.

"Anthony? Are you there? I'm sorry, but at least you have time to plan something."

"Thank you for the information. I'll be in touch."

With a heavy heart, Janice returned to her office to prepare warrants for members of her own family.

Anthony poured a glass of brandy and called Alfonse to explain the situation. He was as dumbfounded as Anthony.

"I need to think about this," Alfonse said. "I'll call you back."

Anthony knew Alfonse wouldn't try to run. He would face the charges. Anthony then called Joe and Phil and told them to meet him immediately at Sam's home. He made a few more calls before leaving the loft.

Sam, Joe, and Phil sat silently, as Anthony told them the news, careful not to mention Janice's name. When he finished, he poured drinks for all of them.

"Now listen carefully," Anthony said. "I long suspected this day would come. I have an attorney in Costa Rica with whom I've been working for over a year. Through him, I made substantial donations to the Costa Rican economy. I also bought a large home on the coast in Playa Conchal, with joint bank accounts with my attorney at the Banco Nacional de Costa Rica.

"My attorney already has citizenship papers prepared for me. Extraditing citizens of Costa Rica to the U.S. is very difficult. The Costa Rican constitution protects its citizens from prosecution for crimes committed outside the country. I told my attorney other family members might join me if we were in danger of prosecution. Citizenship for other people can be arranged.

"There's a JetBlue flight from JFK to Liberia Airport, Costa Rica, tomorrow morning at 11:45. I'll be on that flight, and whoever wants to join me better be there before those warrants can be served. We've got until Monday afternoon, so each of you will have time to transfer funds out of the country first thing in the morning to beat any attempt to freeze your bank accounts."

He gave them the details of the bank he used and explained how to make the transfers.

"I'm in," Sam said.

Anthony looked at Joe and Phil. They faced an incredibly difficult decision, because their mother was in a nursing home.

"We need to think this through," Joe said. "I'll contact you later."

Anthony drove to Daniella's home. While the boys played, he told Daniella he was leaving the country.

"I can't go into details, because I don't want you to be considered an accessory to my crimes. I already bought a home in Costa Rica that's big enough for all of us. Your house is in your name only, so they can't seize it. The mortgage has been paid off. I won't be able to pay any more alimony or child support, though.

"Your options are to remain in Minneola permanently or to wait until the dust settles, then sell the house and bring the boys to live with me in Costa Rica. You can't tell anyone about this. Right now, you can honestly tell the police or the FBI that you didn't know anything about my businesses."

She cried, as he spoke. She couldn't afford a nanny or the house bills if she stayed, and she didn't want the boys growing up without their father.

When she stood, Anthony held her for a long time. Finally, she whispered, "We'll follow you to Costa Rica when the time is right."

Joe and Phil visited the nursing home with their mother, sitting on opposite sides of the bed. They gently woke her, but she was obviously confused and didn't know them.

When Joe tried to explain the situation to her, he began crying and couldn't stop sobbing. She pulled him into her arms and said softly, "It's OK, Giuseppe. Your papa will be home soon. He'll make it better. Don't cry, Little One. Go play with Filippo. Papa will be here soon."

She released him and pulled the covers up around herself before closing her eyes.

Both men wept, knowing it was the last time they would see her.

As Anthony drove toward his home, his cell rang, and caller ID showed it was Beth. He didn't want to speak to her, but he had to for Janice's sake.

"Hi, Beth. I've only got a minute before I reach my parents' house with Sam. We're just about to go inside."

"I understand. Give them my regards."

Anthony was astounded at her calm reply, but he pulled himself together and said good-bye.

He went inside and put as many clothes as he could fit into one large suitcase, then he turned to his files. He already had his personal papers, including birth certificate, marriage and divorce certificates, life insurance, health insurance, and copies of his children's birth certificates and medical papers. To those he added all his financial papers, the deeds of his rental houses, his permanent home, the loft, his U.S. bank account, his offshore accounts, and his Costa Rican accounts.

He added all his contact information and anything else he might need, knowing it was his last chance to bring anything.

He removed photographs from their frames to slide between his clothes. Anything small he wanted to bring went into a second case. The picture of his cherished Grandma Rosa stayed in its frame, though, because she gave him that.

He looked sadly at the car, thinking everything he had of value, be it monetary or sentimental, fit into such a small space. He drove to his parents' home.

Alfonse and Sam were already there. Alfonse told Anthony's parents what was happening, and Anthony was heartbroken to see his father so shaken, while his mother kept crying. When he tried to speak to them, all he could do was nod and close his eyes.

After a while, he announced he had to go, but he carefully didn't mention where he was going, so they wouldn't have to lie to the FBI.

"Once I'm settled, I'll contact you," he said, knowing it wasn't possible.

He hugged his mother, then his father, whispering, "I'm so sorry," to both.

He shook Alfonse's hand. "Don't do anything until Monday evening."

Alfonse nodded. "I'll have my resignation ready."

"Sam, meet me at the agreed place at ten in the morning."

Sam nodded and followed him from the house. When he tried to speak, he couldn't. Shaking his head, he whispered, "This is all my fault."

Anthony held Sam's shoulders and looked him in the eye. "If it wasn't for my own wrongdoing, you never would have been in such a position."

Getting into his car, he drove toward home, stopping at an ATM to withdraw the maximum of $500 in cash.

Back at his house, he prepared the paperwork he would need at the bank when it opened at 8:30AM. After taking one final shower in his own house, he walked through it slowly to photograph every room. He poured a brandy for himself, set his suit on the bed for the following morning, and sat on the sofa, waiting for the next eleven hours to pass.

At 8:30 AM, four men in suits walked into four separate banks in Minneola, New York. Each one asked to transfer all his business, personal, and savings accounts to the Banco Nacional de Costa Rica. Once that was finished, each man drove separately to JFK airport.

Placing their cars in long-term parking, they left the vehicles for the last time. They went through curbside check-in and proceeded to the ticket desk to show their passports.

Once through the security checkpoint, they finally met at Gate A4, shaking hands with each other without speaking.

Their flight boarded on time. The men didn't speak, as they walked down the gangway. A pretty stewardess met them with a smile, as they boarded the jet.

Although it wasn't planned, they all were in first class. Once seated, Anthony called Alfonse and said they would take off on time at 11:45 AM.

"If you don't hear from me by one o'clock, go ahead and hand in your resignation."

Just before takeoff, all four men ordered a brandy to sip, as they left American soil for the foreseeable future.

Elizabeth McLeary was on hold with Judge Terry's Administrative Assistant, Janice Sorrento, who finally returned on the line and apologized for the wait.

"Monday mornings are always crazy," she added.

"What's the status on the warrants I need?" Elizabeth asked.

"They're almost finished, but the judge still has to sign them. He's in court with a complicated case. I'll try to get them signed during one of his breaks, but he'll want to read them over carefully before he affixes his signature. That could take until this evening."

At 12:30 PM. Alfonse checked the JetBlue website to confirm the flight to Costa Rica departed. For his final time as Chief of Police, he drove to City Hall to meet the mayor, who was in a meeting when he arrived.

Much to the secretary's surprise, Alfonse said he would wait.

Thirty minutes later, he sat before the mayor's desk to present his resignation letter, effective immediately.

"What's going on?" the mayor asked, caught totally off-guard.

"I can't say right now, but it will all be clear tomorrow."

"Please stay on until I can find a replacement."

"I'm sorry, but I can't." He set his badge on the desk, stood, shook the mayor's hand, and added, "Thank you for your support all these years."

Alfonse left the building as a private citizen.

The flight to Liberia International Airport took over three hours. When they arrived, Anthony, Sam, Joe, and Phil no longer wore ties or jackets. They collected their luggage and went into Liberia to the office of Attorney Miguel Castillo.

He was expecting them and greeted Anthony with a hug. To the others, he offered a handshake. They took seats, and Consuela, Miguel's secretary brought them bottled water.

"I have contacted the bank about the wire transfers," Miguel began. "Those from Joe and Phil are pending. Once you have finished the paperwork to become Costa Rican citizens, you can go to the bank to open your new accounts."

The first application was relatively simple, asking their demographics, whether there were any criminal charges against them, and if they were involved in drug smuggling. They were able to sign truthfully.

Once the applications were faxed to the Ministry of Immigration, they would be considered pending. All four men finished the paperwork and had it faxed before they left. With their immigration status settled, they could open as many bank accounts as needed.

"I suggest each of you open multiple accounts due to the impending warrants against you from the U.S.," Miguel said. "Because all the money was directed to Anthony's account, he can move them to yours easily."

Once they finished that mammoth task, Miguel took them to Anthony's home in Playa Conchal by limo. Homes were cheaper in Costa Rica, which meant Anthony could afford a magnificent beachfront villa with six bedrooms. The large wall surrounding the house was adorned with deep-pink flowers. Though Anthony had seen pictures, it was the first time he actually visited the property. The others would be able to find homes when they were ready.

Elizabeth, frustrated that the warrants still weren't ready, called Janice again to complain.

"Judge Terry is studying them now," Janice said. "They'll be faxed to you as soon as possible."

Elizabeth ended the call and turned to her team. "Looks like we'll have to wait until tomorrow morning to serve those warrants."

They decided to serve them at 5:30 AM. A team would visit each home of the men to be served. Team 1 would take Anthony's loft. Team 2 would visit the Jackson home. Team 3 would go to Sam's house, and Team 4, led by Elizabeth, would go to Alfonse's home.

All teams would meet in Melville at 4:00 AM.

Ten

Elizabeth still hadn't heard back from Anthony after calling him the previous day. Perhaps he was still busy with Sam. It was easier not to hear from him. She texted him a quick note that she was going to see her aunt at the hospital and would be in touch.

At 4:00 AM, all teams met at the Melville FBI office and were ready. Elizabeth briefed each team on the home they would visit. The only one she didn't know personally from her relationship with Anthony was that of Alfonse Parelli, so she took that assignment.

At 4:00 that morning, Alfonse and Margaret, his wife of twenty-nine years, sat opposite each other at the kitchen table, drinking a cup of coffee with their free hands clasped across the table. They were up all night discussing their future.

As a former Chief of Police, Alfonse knew he faced a long prison sentence. Margaret begged him to flee to Costa Rica, but he refused, and she eventually resigned herself to the fact he might never come home. Both of them knew police officers didn't do well in prison. Initially, they were kept in solitary confinement, but eventually, they were brought into the general population. The case would be well-known with the other inmates, especially the Mexicans, who would seek revenge for his part in planting weapons on a Mexican gang.

He knew the danger, but he felt his decision was correct. Margaret demanded he do the right thing by her and flee together, but he refused to live the rest of his life looking over his shoulder.

They never had children, because Margaret was unable to conceive. They met at City Hall when he'd been a rookie officer. Margaret worked at the Real Estate Tax Office and helped Alfonse find his first home. They married within the year.

Margaret struggled with breast cancer in their early years together. She quit her job and lost the ability to have children. Once she was in remission, she threw herself into volunteering with the homeless and working at the animal sanctuary.

As he supported her through her breast cancer, she supported him throughout his journey from police officer to becoming Chief. She was well-known and well-liked for her volunteer work, as well as for being the Chief's wife.

At 5:30AM, Elizabeth rang the doorbell to the Paselli home and was amazed when Alfonse answered, fully dressed in civilian clothes. He showed no surprise at finding her and three other agents at his front door.

Before she could speak, he opened the door and gestured them inside. Mrs. Paselli sat at the kitchen island, also fully dressed and drinking coffee.

"Chief Alfonse Paselli…." Elizabeth began.

"Actually, Agent McLeary, I'm no longer employed by the department. You may address me as Mr. Paselli."

"Oh." She was caught off guard when he used her real name, as well as by the news of his resignation.

"Well, Alfonse Paselli, I have a warrant signed by Judge Terry for your immediate arrest. You're charged with corruption, violation of civil rights, criminal aiding and abetting, and wrongful arrest and imprisonment."

She recited the Miranda Warning, as a fellow agent walked forward with handcuffs. Elizabeth said quickly, "That won't be necessary."

Mrs. Paselli asked softly, "May I kiss my husband good-bye?"
Elizabeth nodded.

A moment later, the four agents left the home. Elizabeth contacted the other teams for updates and learned that she was the only one who succeeded. The other three homes looked deserted, and no cars were parked outside.

Stunned, she asked, "Repeat, please."

She immediately realized their undercover operation was no secret, and that all five men knew they were coming. Furious, she tried to think who at the agency could have leaked the information.

She recalled her recent phone conversation and message with Anthony and realized he had known for some time.

"Mr. Paselli, where are the other four men?" she asked.
"I don't know," he replied honestly.

Back at the FBI office, as Alfonse was being processed, Elizabeth called the banks where each of the suspects had bank accounts, but only one was open at eight o'clock. She identified herself to the bank manager, and he confirmed he received the faxed warrants to freeze the accounts of Phil and Joe Jackson, as well as any accounts associated with Jackson Construction.

"I'm sorry, Agent, but those accounts were closed yesterday. The funds were wired to a bank in Costa Rica."

Stunned and livid, she realized none of the other bank accounts would still be in existence, either.

She immediately called a team meeting. Once all were assembled, she spoke to them angrily, her face almost as red as her hair.

"Who talked about this case outside this office?" she demanded.

No one admitted it.

"Each of you will be investigated by the Office of Professional Responsibility!" She stormed from the room and went to her own office, slamming the door behind her.

She knew her boss, Assistant Special Agent in Charge Tony Kuertz would call soon, but she didn't expect him to barge through her door.

"Why are all those agents being turned over to OPR?" he asked.

To her surprise and horror, she burst into tears.

"Jesus, Elizabeth! What's going on?" he asked softly, sitting in front of her desk.

"I'm so sorry. I can't believe I just did that. I've been doing this job for years, and I can't believe what just happened. I'm annoyed, embarrassed, and frustrated."

"What happened?"

She told him the story but omitted the part where she became emotionally involved with Anthony.

Once he heard four of the men had fled the country and taken all their funds, he was livid, too. "I want to interview Anthony Paselli with you."

They had Paselli brought into an interview room.

"You know me," Elizabeth began. "This is Assistant Special Agent in Charge Tony Kuertz. Please describe your involvement in the arrests of Carlos, Andreas, and Miguel Martinez."

"No comment."

"How did you know your arrest was imminent?"

"You have a rat on your team."

"You'd better talk for your own sake," Tony said.

Alfonse merely smiled. "You should remember who you're talking to."

Thirty minutes later, Alfonse was escorted back to his cell.

Team members worked frantically to trace the movements of Anthony Vito, Samuel Garillo, and Philip and Joseph Jackson. They soon learned that all the men appeared at their banks at 8:30 AM Monday morning and wired money to the Banco Nacional of Costa Rica.

Other team members discovered that all four boarded a JetBlue flight that departed JFK to Liberia International Airport in Costa Rica at 11:45 AM the same day. When they contacted the American Embassy in San José, Costa Rica, embassy staff confirmed the arrival of all four and promised to search for them.

An arraignment hearing for Anthony Paselli was scheduled for four o'clock that afternoon. Alfonse, waiving his right to an attorney, stood alone before the judge.

The judge read the charges to him. "How do you plead?"

"No contest, Your Honor."

"You understand the consequences of not going to trial? Is anyone forcing you to take that plea?"

"I'm aware of the consequences, Your Honor. Based on my knowledge of the law, I will stick with a plea of no contest."

"I remand this prisoner into custody to await sentencing," the judge said.

Before Elizabeth left the office for the evening, she contacted the American Embassy in Costa Rica and spoke to an official named Marco Gonzales.

"We've only just begun our investigations," Marco said. "Anthony is very popular with Costa Rican officials due to his generous contributions to the economy. We'll be in touch once we know more."

Eleven

The following morning, after a sleepless night, Elizabeth spoke to ASAC Tony Kuertz.

"I feel responsible for Anthony's sudden departure. I don't know how the leak happened, but I'm convinced it's my fault. I'd like to request a temporary assignment to the American Embassy FBI office in Costa Rica. I know this case better than anyone, and I need to do this."

"All right. I'll make the calls."

Elizabeth took the same flight, JetBlue from JFK at 11:45 AM to Liberia, as Anthony and the others took the previous day. A car met her at the airport and drove her the three-and-a-half hours to the embassy in San José. She briefly met Marco Gonzales before being taken to the Isla Verde Hotel to check in. During the brief stop at the embassy, Marco told her the legal ramifications of extradition from Costa Rica to the U.S.

Elizabeth ordered room service and sat on the small balcony overlooking San José's Pavas District. As she pored over the paperwork, she felt increasingly positive about beginning extradition proceedings against the four men.

The following day, her positivity took a nosedive when she heard from Marco that all four applied for Costa Rican citizenship.

Due to Anthony's generous donations, Marco said there was little doubt citizenship would be quickly granted.

"Their immigration cases are pending right now," Marco added. "Because of that, the authorities will protect them from extradition. All such cases must be presented to the Justice Department's Office of International Affairs for approval. The first hurdle is for the Justice Department to determine if the fugitive is extraditable. Although we have a Treaty of Extradition between our countries, Costa Rica fiercely protects its citizens against extradition for crimes committed away from Costa Rican soil. The International Affairs Justice Department won't approve extradition if there is any reason to deny it. In this case, with Anthony's previous financial contributions, the fact that the crimes are nonviolent, and the four have pending citizenships, it's unlikely any extradition requests will be honored."

Elizabeth was astounded. Finding a small office with a desk available, she called ASAC Tony Kuertz and told him the news.

"You should come back," he advised. "We'll present the case to the Justice Department's Office of International Affairs in New York."

Once back in New York, Elizabeth immersed herself on all available information concerning Costa Rican extradition. She spoke to prosecutors across the country who either succeeded or failed in that process. Although she no longer felt confident, she helped prepare the case and submitted it for approval by the Justice Department's Office on International Affairs.

She waited for three weeks to hear the decision. As predicated, the four men were eventually ruled as non-extraditable. She was devastated. The only way to arrest them was if they left Costa Rican soil.

Alfonse Paselli pleaded no contest to the charges, which meant he couldn't be interviewed again, and he was merely awaiting his sentence. The case was over unless they found the person who leaked the news of the raids to the four escaped men.

Elizabeth barged into Tony's office, and he sat back in his chair to listen. After explaining her intense disappointment about the results of the case, she asked, "May I speak freely and off the record?"

"Of course."

"I had a romantic relationship with Anthony." She blushed.

"Why are you telling me this?"

"I feel I can convince him to come back to the U.S. if I'm given permission to follow him to Costa Rica. I understand I can't go as an FBI agent, but if I show up as a private citizen, I can rekindle the relationship and bring him back."

For the first time in many years, Tony was speechless. It was clear Elizabeth was far too involved in the case and wasn't thinking rationally.

"You need to understand the ramifications of your request," he said slowly. "Even though you wouldn't be working for the FBI, the Costa Rican government can hold you accountable, because you were the lead and undercover agent in the case. That could further impede any chance we have to get those men back.

"You need a break, Elizabeth. I want you to take one week off at full pay to get your life back together."

Disappointed, she returned to her apartment in Melville, where she packed a bag and booked a ticket for the following day's flight from JFK to Liberia.

Unlike the fugitives she followed, Elizabeth sat in coach on a crowded flight. When she arrived in Costa Rica, she got a rental car and drove to Playa Conchal, not San José. She booked a room in a small hotel far from the beach to save money.

After tossing her suitcase on the bed, she set out to find the home where the four fugitives lived. She drove slowly along the beach boulevard until she found the address, but the home was hidden behind a white wall covered in pink flowers with a locked iron gate.

Unwilling to give up, she parked the car and walked along the beach until she found the sprawling home from that side. She wore a large, floppy hat with sunglasses, so she felt comfortable walking closer to examine the house.

Although surrounded by a tall wall and wrought-iron gate, it had easy beach access. The large, opulent villa had windows along the entire beach side of the house. A large lanai had three pools connected by small waterways, with an elegant waterfall of large white boulders at one end of the pool, with a slide at the opposite end. A covered tiki bar could be accessed either from the water or the lanai. Beside the pool was a large spa shaded by a palm tree.

She never saw anything like it. She hurried back to her car and returned to the hotel to document everything she saw before raiding the vending machine in the hotel lobby and the minibar in her room.

The following day, she returned to the beach in front of Anthony's home. Wearing her hat and sunglasses, she walked the beach, hoping to glimpse someone inside. She thought she saw Anthony swimming in the ocean, but a closer look revealed it was someone else.

Walking up to the rear of the property, she looked through the wrought-iron gate on that side. As she peered in, someone tapped her shoulder.

She turned and saw Anthony behind her in swimming trunks. He opened his mouth to speak, then recognized her and stopped.

They stared at each other without speaking. Finally, she turned to walk away.

"Beth, come back!" he shouted.

She dealt with several emotions simultaneously. The predominant and most uncomfortable was intense desire. Turning slowly, she walked back. When they were face-to-face, she wondered if her knees might buckle, as her face flushed.

He placed his hands on her shoulders. "Beth, or would you prefer Elizabeth?" He cocked his head and smiled.

"Beth's fine," she whispered. "That's what my parents call me."

"I guess they aren't dead, then."

"No."

"My feelings for you haven't changed. Obviously, the situation is different now. You know all about me, but I know almost nothing about you except your job. I did things I'm not proud of. What started off innocently enough to keep the mayor off my back mushroomed and turned me into a criminal, someone I don't recognize or like.

"I've destroyed many lives and broken my parents' hearts. I placed Alfonse into a hell I can't imagine. Phil and Joe will never see their mother again, and she'll die alone. I'm a monster. You put a stop to that horrific behavior, and I'm grateful. I'm glad I can tell you this in person."

"Then come home and face the courts like Alfonse."

"I can't do that, Beth. I have two children to worry about, and Sam needs a lot of care, too. His being involved in this disaster is my fault. I made a lot of money in those scams, and I intend to pay it all back. I have the records of everything I took. Once I figure things out, I'll return every penny. They have my house and loft back home, plus my car. That'll help. I'll keep the rest to look after the boys, Daniella, Sam, and, perhaps, you."

"You can't be serious."

"I'm deathly serious."

"I'm an FBI agent. I took an oath to uphold the law. My job is to get you back to the States to face your crimes and pay your debt to society. For God's sake, Anthony, you abused your position and took advantage of the elderly!"

"I know I'm a monster. The situation got out of hand, then it got worse and worse. Then other people became involved, and I need to protect them. I won't go home, Beth. I'll repay my debt to Minneola, but that's where I stop. I can't return home, and that's punishment in itself."

"You don't really think you're being punished when you live in a mansion on the beach? What about Alfonse? Will you really let him take the hit for all of you?"

"I talked to him at length before I left. I didn't agree with his choice, but I respect it. Beth, I have to meet my attorney. Please, can we talk later? I have so much I need to say, to explain, to you. Can we meet at the Sandbar Restaurant for dinner around eight? Would that work?"

She nodded and walked away.

"Beth!" he shouted.

She turned, and he tried to take her in his arms. She pulled away. "I'll see you later to talk. That's all we'll be doing."

As she passed the front desk of her hotel, the manager waved a piece of paper to get her attention. It was a message from ASAC Tony Kuertz that read, *Call me.*

Beth went to her room and collapsed on the bed, her head spinning. Closing her eyes, she tried to make sense of what happened. Coming to Costa Rica was a mistake, as Tony said, but she needed to decide what to do next. She decided against calling Tony. It was her problem, and she had to face it.

Why on earth did Anthony think she would stay with him? He was a fugitive running from the law, and she was an FBI agent following him while also pursuing a romantic relationship. It was absurd.

She should never have come to Costa Rica. She should have listened to Tony. She would call Anthony and cancel their appointment.

She remembered she didn't have his number. She had to tell him in person she was going home, and if he wanted a relationship, he needed to come with her.

Filled with emotional turmoil, she fell into a fitful sleep.

She woke to the sound of the phone ringing. Answering it groggily, she regretted the impulse when she heard Tony's voice. She kept saying, "Hello?" repeatedly, as if unable to hear him, then she hung up.

As she showered, she heard the phone ringing constantly. The sound of the dryer on her hair helped drown out the phone. It took more time than usual to put on her makeup and sweep her hair back into a clip. She wore a short, elegant black dress, and black sandals with short heels. When she was ready, she asked the hotel manager to call a cab for her.

She arrived at the Sandbar just before eight o'clock and reminded herself she was a strong, confident woman, a professional, but her heart felt like that of a giddy teenager. Her brain told her to run, but her heart told her to stay.

She glanced for Anthony, as she walked to the bar, then a warm hand touched her shoulder, and her heart beat so fast, it was ready to burst. She turned and saw him in cream cotton slacks, a black cotton shirt, and cream sandals. His dark, wet hair was combed back.

Her knees threatened to give way, as she shook her head. He took her hand and guided her to a small table on the beach outdoor patio. The full moon cast a romantic glow over them, aided by the flickering candle on the table.

"I shouldn't be here with you," Beth said. "I came to plead that you'd do the right thing. I don't know what I was thinking when I agreed to meet you for dinner. You're a fugitive running from the law in a foreign country. You're everything I don't believe in. You're the epitome of the kind of criminal I've spent my entire adult life trying to bring to justice."

"Yet here we are. Beth, I fell in love with you. At the time, I didn't know who you were. When I realized you were an FBI agent, I tried to hate you, but I couldn't. In fact, you set me free. I created an impossible situation that had to end. You ended it, and for that, I'll be eternally grateful. I believe I love you more now than before."

"Shit! That doesn't help. I'm trying to tell you this is an absurd situation. I can't do this. I've spent years working to get where I am now. Damn it, I love what I do, and I'm good at it. I can't and won't throw it all away. Anthony, what do you want of me?"

The waiter brought two tropical drinks Anthony ordered. Beth, thirsty from the heat, drank the sweet liquid quickly.

"Be careful," Anthony warned. "Tropical drinks are notoriously full of rum."

She immediately felt the effects, and, for the first time that evening, she smiled.

"Give me a chance," he pleaded. "I have a week to convince you that you love me. What we had was special. I never felt that way before, not even with the mother of my children. Stay here with me in Costa Rica. Let's spend the week together. Then you can go back home to work and decide. Can you do that?"

"Absolutely not." She flagged the water for a refill.

They ordered dinner, and Anthony discussed his plans. He spoke about the agony Phil and Joe felt leaving their mother behind in the States. He added Sam was doing well and was back to his jovial self. He didn't remember much about the night he overdosed and was still in therapy, speaking with the therapist in Florida via FaceTime.

"Daniella and the boys will move down here eventually. I'm looking for a house for them nearby. I miss them and speak to the boys every day."

When he discussed his parents, tears came to his eyes. Along with some aunts and uncles, his parents were already planning a trip to Costa Rica.

Beth, feeling tipsy from the alcohol, told him about herself. What he learned earlier was just her cover story. She was born in West Chester, and her parents were still alive. She pursued her dream of becoming an FBI agent and eventually went to the FBI Academy in Quantico.

She became a supervisor, and her next logical step would be Assistant Special Agent in Charge, ASOC. She explained her life as an only child and how her parents supported her throughout her life. Like Anthony, she loved being out on the water—kayaking, boating, swimming—anything to do with water sports.

He promised to take her parasailing off the beach, and she enthusiastically agreed.

After dinner, they walked along the beach barefoot. Anthony held her hand. She tried to remove it, then shrugged and left it there. She had a deep feeling of security and passion, as they walked.

Eventually, they reached the beach gate to Anthony's new home. He invited her in, but she refused.

"I need to get back to the hotel to gather my thoughts." She also knew she needed to sober up and get back to reality, as well as call Tony Kuertz in the morning.

Anthony drove her to her hotel and kissed her forehead before leaving.

Beth couldn't sleep. Too many scenarios competed in her mind. She went back to her training and got out of bed, grabbing paper from her case to write down all the reasons she shouldn't fall in love with Anthony Vito.

By four o'clock in the morning, she fell asleep on a bed strewn with papers depicting the many possible roles her life could take.

She woke when the phone rang at eight.

"I've arranged for us to go parasailing at eleven-thirty this morning," Anthony said. "I'll pick you up around eleven."

"OK." She hung up, then she dialed Tony Kuertz in New York.

He was clearly annoyed. "I gave you the week off to rest, not chase fugitives in Costa Rica."

"This is something I have to do, not only in my capacity as a Special Agent but personally."

He was silent for a second, feeling flabbergasted. "I must have misheard you. I expect you back in this office on Monday."

Before the call ended, his voice softened. "Please be careful. Think this through and call my personal cell if you need anything."

500 feet above the coastline of western Costa Rica, Beth held Anthony's hand in a death grip, as they parasailed over the beach and ocean. The water was a clear, Caribbean aqua. The shore was littered with people paddling and swimming. Beach umbrellas of all colors dotted the sand.

Farther offshore, they saw large fish, then a school of sharks that were within fifty feet of the beach.

Beth pointed them out, and Anthony nodded, gesturing that he wasn't swimming in the ocean anymore.

When they landed, they headed for a beach bar they saw from above. Sipping Piña Coladas in the warm sunshine, they waited for their orders of shrimp and lobster to be served.

After paying the barman, they walked and chatted along the beach until they came to his house. Beth hesitated.

"The guys know you're in town and bear you no malice," he said.

Once through the gate, he gave her a tour of the place. No one else was home, which made her feel more comfortable. Still feeling mellow from the Piña Coladas, Anthony led her to the master bedroom.

"I need to shower." He removed his clothes.

She did the same and followed him. Steamy water poured over them, as they kissed passionately.

Anthony scooped her into his arms and carried her into the bedroom. Still wet from the shower, they made passionate love on the bed. She felt an intense bond she never felt before.

Exhausted, they slept entangled in each other's arms.

They awoke the following morning to sunlight streaming through the window. She didn't bring any clothes, so she wore only a swimsuit and cover-up when she met Sam, Joe, and Phil. They looked at each other in awkward silence for a moment.

"Would you like coffee?" Joe asked.

Sam hugged her.

"Is it Beth or Elizabeth?" Phil asked with a grin.

Beth inquired about their mother and promised to visit her when she returned to New York. She also promised to contact them via FaceTime during the visit.

Anthony took her back to her hotel.

As they drove, she asked, "Will you return to the States with me? You can do your prison time, then we can be together once you're free."

"I'm facing thirty years of incarceration. It would be a lifetime without you. I'm serious about returning all the money, but I won't go to prison. Will you visit my attorney with me?"

The look on Miguel Castillo's face was priceless when Anthony introduced Beth as the lead FBI investigator on his case.

Anthony explained how they met and that he loved her. "I've asked her to live with me here in Costa Rica."

Miguel and Beth were speechless. Miguel slowly opened a cabinet under his desk and took out a bottle of Scotch and three glasses. After they all had one shot, Miguel had two more.

"I have no intention of remaining in Costa Rica," Beth said.

Miguel nodded. "There isn't much that catches me off guard anymore, but Anthony has brought me the most-fascinating case I ever had."

"I won't move down here."

"If you ever change your mind, you could find a similar position in Costa Rica and would be an invaluable employee with your knowledge of the American legal system and its politics."

On the way to Playa Conchal, Anthony said, "Please spend the rest of your vacation with me, so you can be absolutely sure you want to go back to New York."

"All right, but I must have my own bedroom."

Back at the house, Beth lounged by the pool, as Anthony swam laps, splashing her each time he went past. She repaid him by jumping into the pool in front of him.

They frolicked like teenagers before sitting in the hot, bubbly spa with salty margaritas. Phil and Joe joined them, as the sun set. Sam remained indoors to prepare dinner.

The week passed quickly, and Beth soon was on a JetBlue flight back to New York. Her first stop upon landing was to visit her parents in West Chester. They listened intently, as she described the last six months of her life. Somehow, a bottle of Scotch appeared, as they tried to understand the confusing situation.

"So what do you intend to do?" her father asked.

"Actually, I came to you for advice."

"You need to follow your gut," her mother said. "You're in love with this man, and your relationship has already survived the unbelievable. In my opinion, love like that comes only once in a lifetime. You have to think it over very carefully."

"Beth, you completed some grueling work to become a Special Agent," her father said. "No matter what, I'll support your decision."

Beth returned home feeling none the wiser and more confused than ever.

The following day was more enlightening, as she sat in front of Tony Kuertz, the ASAC for Suffolk County. Incredulous, Tony couldn't believe Beth followed Anthony to Costa Rica. Even worse, she was thinking of joining him. It was beyond Tony's comprehension.

"He's everything you have fought against for your entire career," Tony said. "He's a criminal, a con man, a fugitive from the law, a coward, someone who took advantage of the elderly, and he was considered one of the most-valuable citizens of his community."

When Beth tried to explain Anthony's situation, Tony stared in disbelief.

"Will you think about what you just said?" Tony asked. "If word gets out about any of this, your FBI career is over. You could even be breaking the law just by living with him, essentially condoning his behavior. You could be charged with aiding and abetting a crime.

"If we ever manage to extradite him, what will you do? You need to go home without saying a word about this to anyone. Come back in when you're in your right mind. I'll cover for you by saying you're ill."

That night, she called Anthony and told him she wasn't going to join him in Costa Rica. As the connection fell silent, she felt sick to her stomach. He hadn't hung up, and she could only imagine how upset he was.

"I think it's best if we don't speak again," she said, ending the call.

She wept silently when she crawled into bed. Although emotionally and physically exhausted, sleep eluded her.

Still in bed the following day, she barely ate anything. Miserable and desperately missing Anthony, she kept going over what Tony Kuertz told her, trying to convince herself she made the right decision.

She considered calling Anthony back only to decide against it.

When Tony called, she agreed to come back to work the following day.

"You've got a complicated case waiting for you that should keep your mind busy," he said.

Twelve

The following morning, after a sleepless night, Elizabeth spoke to ASAC Tony Kuertz.

"I feel responsible for Anthony's sudden departure. I don't know how the leak happened, but I'm convinced it's my fault. I'd like to request a temporary assignment to the American Embassy FBI office in Costa Rica. I know this case better than anyone, and I need to do this."

"All right. I'll make the calls."

Elizabeth took the same flight, JetBlue from JFK at 11:45 AM to Liberia, as Anthony and the others took the previous day. A car met her at the airport and drove her the three-and-a-half hours to the embassy in San José. She briefly met Marco Gonzales before being taken to the Isla Verde Hotel to check in. During the brief stop at the embassy, Marco told her the legal ramifications of extradition from Costa Rica to the U.S.

Elizabeth ordered room service and sat on the small balcony overlooking San José's Pavas District. As she pored over the paperwork, she felt increasingly positive about beginning extradition proceedings against the four men.

The following day, her positivity took a nosedive when she heard from Marco that all four applied for Costa Rican citizenship.

Due to Anthony's generous donations, Marco said there was little doubt citizenship would be quickly granted.

"Their immigration cases are pending right now," Marco added. "Because of that, the authorities will protect them from extradition. All such cases must be presented to the Justice Department's Office of International Affairs for approval. The first hurdle is for the Justice Department to determine if the fugitive is extraditable. Although we have a Treaty of Extradition between our countries, Costa Rica fiercely protects its citizens against extradition for crimes committed away from Costa Rican soil. The International Affairs Justice Department won't approve extradition if there is any reason to deny it. In this case, with Anthony's previous financial contributions, the fact that the crimes are nonviolent, and the four have pending citizenships, it's unlikely any extradition requests will be honored."

Elizabeth was astounded. Finding a small office with a desk available, she called ASAC Tony Kuertz and told him the news.

"You should come back," he advised. "We'll present the case to the Justice Department's Office of International Affairs in New York."

Once back in New York, Elizabeth immersed herself on all available information concerning Costa Rican extradition. She spoke to prosecutors across the country who either succeeded or failed in that process. Although she no longer felt confident, she helped prepare the case and submitted it for approval by the Justice Department's Office on International Affairs.

She waited for three weeks to hear the decision. As predicated, the four men were eventually ruled as non-extraditable. She was devastated. The only way to arrest them was if they left Costa Rican soil.

Alfonse Paselli pleaded no contest to the charges, which meant he couldn't be interviewed again, and he was merely awaiting his sentence. The case was over unless they found the person who leaked the news of the raids to the four escaped men.

Elizabeth barged into Tony's office, and he sat back in his chair to listen. After explaining her intense disappointment about the results of the case, she asked, "May I speak freely and off the record?"

"Of course."

"I had a romantic relationship with Anthony." She blushed.

"Why are you telling me this?"

"I feel I can convince him to come back to the U.S. if I'm given permission to follow him to Costa Rica. I understand I can't go as an FBI agent, but if I show up as a private citizen, I can rekindle the relationship and bring him back."

For the first time in many years, Tony was speechless. It was clear Elizabeth was far too involved in the case and wasn't thinking rationally.

"You need to understand the ramifications of your request," he said slowly. "Even though you wouldn't be working for the FBI, the Costa Rican government can hold you accountable, because you were the lead and undercover agent in the case. That could further impede any chance we have to get those men back.

"You need a break, Elizabeth. I want you to take one week off at full pay to get your life back together."

Disappointed, she returned to her apartment in Melville, where she packed a bag and booked a ticket for the following day's flight from JFK to Liberia.

Unlike the fugitives she followed, Elizabeth sat in coach on a crowded flight. When she arrived in Costa Rica, she got a rental car and drove to Playa Conchal, not San José. She booked a room in a small hotel far from the beach to save money.

After tossing her suitcase on the bed, she set out to find the home where the four fugitives lived. She drove slowly along the beach boulevard until she found the address, but the home was hidden behind a white wall covered in pink flowers with a locked iron gate.

Unwilling to give up, she parked the car and walked along the beach until she found the sprawling home from that side. She wore a large, floppy hat with sunglasses, so she felt comfortable walking closer to examine the house.

Although surrounded by a tall wall and wrought-iron gate, it had easy beach access. The large, opulent villa had windows along the entire beach side of the house. A large lanai had three pools connected by small waterways, with an elegant waterfall of large white boulders at one end of the pool, with a slide at the opposite end. A covered tiki bar could be accessed either from the water or the lanai. Beside the pool was a large spa shaded by a palm tree.

She never saw anything like it. She hurried back to her car and returned to the hotel to document everything she saw before raiding the vending machine in the hotel lobby and the minibar in her room.

The following day, she returned to the beach in front of Anthony's home. Wearing her hat and sunglasses, she walked the beach, hoping to glimpse someone inside. She thought she saw Anthony swimming in the ocean, but a closer look revealed it was someone else.

Walking up to the rear of the property, she looked through the wrought-iron gate on that side. As she peered in, someone tapped her shoulder.

She turned and saw Anthony behind her in swimming trunks. He opened his mouth to speak, then recognized her and stopped.

They stared at each other without speaking. Finally, she turned to walk away.

"Beth, come back!" he shouted.

She dealt with several emotions simultaneously. The predominant and most uncomfortable was intense desire. Turning slowly, she walked back. When they were face-to-face, she wondered if her knees might buckle, as her face flushed.

He placed his hands on her shoulders. "Beth, or would you prefer Elizabeth?" He cocked his head and smiled.

"Beth's fine," she whispered. "That's what my parents call me."

"I guess they aren't dead, then."

"No."

"My feelings for you haven't changed. Obviously, the situation is different now. You know all about me, but I know almost nothing about you except your job. I did things I'm not proud of. What started off innocently enough to keep the mayor off my back mushroomed and turned me into a criminal, someone I don't recognize or like.

"I've destroyed many lives and broken my parents' hearts. I placed Alfonse into a hell I can't imagine. Phil and Joe will never see their mother again, and she'll die alone. I'm a monster. You put a stop to that horrific behavior, and I'm grateful. I'm glad I can tell you this in person."

"Then come home and face the courts like Alfonse."

"I can't do that, Beth. I have two children to worry about, and Sam needs a lot of care, too. His being involved in this disaster is my fault. I made a lot of money in those scams, and I intend to pay it all back. I have the records of everything I took. Once I figure things out, I'll return every penny. They have my house and loft back home, plus my car. That'll help. I'll keep the rest to look after the boys, Daniella, Sam, and, perhaps, you."

"You can't be serious."

"I'm deathly serious."

"I'm an FBI agent. I took an oath to uphold the law. My job is to get you back to the States to face your crimes and pay your debt to society. For God's sake, Anthony, you abused your position and took advantage of the elderly!"

"I know I'm a monster. The situation got out of hand, then it got worse and worse. Then other people became involved, and I need to protect them. I won't go home, Beth. I'll repay my debt to Minneola, but that's where I stop. I can't return home, and that's punishment in itself."

"You don't really think you're being punished when you live in a mansion on the beach? What about Alfonse? Will you really let him take the hit for all of you?"

"I talked to him at length before I left. I didn't agree with his choice, but I respect it. Beth, I have to meet my attorney. Please, can we talk later? I have so much I need to say, to explain, to you. Can we meet at the Sandbar Restaurant for dinner around eight? Would that work?"

She nodded and walked away.

"Beth!" he shouted.

She turned, and he tried to take her in his arms. She pulled away. "I'll see you later to talk. That's all we'll be doing."

As she passed the front desk of her hotel, the manager waved a piece of paper to get her attention. It was a message from ASAC Tony Kuertz that read, *Call me.*

Beth went to her room and collapsed on the bed, her head spinning. Closing her eyes, she tried to make sense of what happened. Coming to Costa Rica was a mistake, as Tony said, but she needed to decide what to do next. She decided against calling Tony. It was her problem, and she had to face it.

Why on earth did Anthony think she would stay with him? He was a fugitive running from the law, and she was an FBI agent following him while also pursuing a romantic relationship. It was absurd.

She should never have come to Costa Rica. She should have listened to Tony. She would call Anthony and cancel their appointment.

She remembered she didn't have his number. She had to tell him in person she was going home, and if he wanted a relationship, he needed to come with her.

Filled with emotional turmoil, she fell into a fitful sleep.

She woke to the sound of the phone ringing. Answering it groggily, she regretted the impulse when she heard Tony's voice. She kept saying, "Hello?" repeatedly, as if unable to hear him, then she hung up.

As she showered, she heard the phone ringing constantly. The sound of the dryer on her hair helped drown out the phone. It took more time than usual to put on her makeup and sweep her hair back into a clip. She wore a short, elegant black dress, and black sandals with short heels. When she was ready, she asked the hotel manager to call a cab for her.

She arrived at the Sandbar just before eight o'clock and reminded herself she was a strong, confident woman, a professional, but her heart felt like that of a giddy teenager. Her brain told her to run, but her heart told her to stay.

She glanced for Anthony, as she walked to the bar, then a warm hand touched her shoulder, and her heart beat so fast, it was ready to burst. She turned and saw him in cream cotton slacks, a black cotton shirt, and cream sandals. His dark, wet hair was combed back.

Her knees threatened to give way, as she shook her head. He took her hand and guided her to a small table on the beach outdoor patio. The full moon cast a romantic glow over them, aided by the flickering candle on the table.

"I shouldn't be here with you," Beth said. "I came to plead that you'd do the right thing. I don't know what I was thinking when I agreed to meet you for dinner. You're a fugitive running from the law in a foreign country. You're everything I don't believe in. You're the epitome of the kind of criminal I've spent my entire adult life trying to bring to justice."

"Yet here we are. Beth, I fell in love with you. At the time, I didn't know who you were. When I realized you were an FBI agent, I tried to hate you, but I couldn't. In fact, you set me free. I created an impossible situation that had to end. You ended it, and for that, I'll be eternally grateful. I believe I love you more now than before."

"Shit! That doesn't help. I'm trying to tell you this is an absurd situation. I can't do this. I've spent years working to get where I am now. Damn it, I love what I do, and I'm good at it. I can't and won't throw it all away. Anthony, what do you want of me?"

The waiter brought two tropical drinks Anthony ordered. Beth, thirsty from the heat, drank the sweet liquid quickly.

"Be careful," Anthony warned. "Tropical drinks are notoriously full of rum."

She immediately felt the effects, and, for the first time that evening, she smiled.

"Give me a chance," he pleaded. "I have a week to convince you that you love me. What we had was special. I never felt that way before, not even with the mother of my children. Stay here with me in Costa Rica. Let's spend the week together. Then you can go back home to work and decide. Can you do that?"

"Absolutely not." She flagged the water for a refill.

They ordered dinner, and Anthony discussed his plans. He spoke about the agony Phil and Joe felt leaving their mother behind in the States. He added Sam was doing well and was back to his jovial self. He didn't remember much about the night he overdosed and was still in therapy, speaking with the therapist in Florida via FaceTime.

"Daniella and the boys will move down here eventually. I'm looking for a house for them nearby. I miss them and speak to the boys every day."

When he discussed his parents, tears came to his eyes. Along with some aunts and uncles, his parents were already planning a trip to Costa Rica.

Beth, feeling tipsy from the alcohol, told him about herself. What he learned earlier was just her cover story. She was born in West Chester, and her parents were still alive. She pursued her dream of becoming an FBI agent and eventually went to the FBI Academy in Quantico.

She became a supervisor, and her next logical step would be Assistant Special Agent in Charge, ASOC. She explained her life as an only child and how her parents supported her throughout her life. Like Anthony, she loved being out on the water—kayaking, boating, swimming—anything to do with water sports.

He promised to take her parasailing off the beach, and she enthusiastically agreed.

After dinner, they walked along the beach barefoot. Anthony held her hand. She tried to remove it, then shrugged and left it there. She had a deep feeling of security and passion, as they walked.

Eventually, they reached the beach gate to Anthony's new home. He invited her in, but she refused.

"I need to get back to the hotel to gather my thoughts." She also knew she needed to sober up and get back to reality, as well as call Tony Kuertz in the morning.

Anthony drove her to her hotel and kissed her forehead before leaving.

Beth couldn't sleep. Too many scenarios competed in her mind. She went back to her training and got out of bed, grabbing paper from her case to write down all the reasons she shouldn't fall in love with Anthony Vito.

By four o'clock in the morning, she fell asleep on a bed strewn with papers depicting the many possible roles her life could take.

She woke when the phone rang at eight.

"I've arranged for us to go parasailing at eleven-thirty this morning," Anthony said. "I'll pick you up around eleven."

"OK." She hung up, then she dialed Tony Kuertz in New York.

He was clearly annoyed. "I gave you the week off to rest, not chase fugitives in Costa Rica."

"This is something I have to do, not only in my capacity as a Special Agent but personally."

He was silent for a second, feeling flabbergasted. "I must have misheard you. I expect you back in this office on Monday."

Before the call ended, his voice softened. "Please be careful. Think this through and call my personal cell if you need anything."

500 feet above the coastline of western Costa Rica, Beth held Anthony's hand in a death grip, as they parasailed over the beach and ocean. The water was a clear, Caribbean aqua. The shore was littered with people paddling and swimming. Beach umbrellas of all colors dotted the sand.

Farther offshore, they saw large fish, then a school of sharks that were within fifty feet of the beach.

Beth pointed them out, and Anthony nodded, gesturing that he wasn't swimming in the ocean anymore.

When they landed, they headed for a beach bar they saw from above. Sipping Piña Coladas in the warm sunshine, they waited for their orders of shrimp and lobster to be served.

After paying the barman, they walked and chatted along the beach until they came to his house. Beth hesitated.

"The guys know you're in town and bear you no malice," he said.

Once through the gate, he gave her a tour of the place. No one else was home, which made her feel more comfortable. Still feeling mellow from the Piña Coladas, Anthony led her to the master bedroom.

"I need to shower." He removed his clothes.

She did the same and followed him. Steamy water poured over them, as they kissed passionately.

Anthony scooped her into his arms and carried her into the bedroom. Still wet from the shower, they made passionate love on the bed. She felt an intense bond she never felt before.

Exhausted, they slept entangled in each other's arms.

They awoke the following morning to sunlight streaming through the window. She didn't bring any clothes, so she wore only a swimsuit and cover-up when she met Sam, Joe, and Phil. They looked at each other in awkward silence for a moment.

"Would you like coffee?" Joe asked.

Sam hugged her.

"Is it Beth or Elizabeth?" Phil asked with a grin.

Beth inquired about their mother and promised to visit her when she returned to New York. She also promised to contact them via FaceTime during the visit.

Anthony took her back to her hotel.

As they drove, she asked, "Will you return to the States with me? You can do your prison time, then we can be together once you're free."

"I'm facing thirty years of incarceration. It would be a lifetime without you. I'm serious about returning all the money, but I won't go to prison. Will you visit my attorney with me?"

The look on Miguel Castillo's face was priceless when Anthony introduced Beth as the lead FBI investigator on his case.

Anthony explained how they met and that he loved her. "I've asked her to live with me here in Costa Rica."

Miguel and Beth were speechless. Miguel slowly opened a cabinet under his desk and took out a bottle of Scotch and three glasses. After they all had one shot, Miguel had two more.

"I have no intention of remaining in Costa Rica," Beth said.

Miguel nodded. "There isn't much that catches me off guard anymore, but Anthony has brought me the most-fascinating case I ever had."

"I won't move down here."

"If you ever change your mind, you could find a similar position in Costa Rica and would be an invaluable employee with your knowledge of the American legal system and its politics."

On the way to Playa Conchal, Anthony said, "Please spend the rest of your vacation with me, so you can be absolutely sure you want to go back to New York."

"All right, but I must have my own bedroom."

Back at the house, Beth lounged by the pool, as Anthony swam laps, splashing her each time he went past. She repaid him by jumping into the pool in front of him.

They frolicked like teenagers before sitting in the hot, bubbly spa with salty margaritas. Phil and Joe joined them, as the sun set. Sam remained indoors to prepare dinner.

The week passed quickly, and Beth soon was on a JetBlue flight back to New York. Her first stop upon landing was to visit her parents in West Chester. They listened intently, as she described the last six months of her life. Somehow, a bottle of Scotch appeared, as they tried to understand the confusing situation.

"So what do you intend to do?" her father asked.

"Actually, I came to you for advice."

"You need to follow your gut," her mother said. "You're in love with this man, and your relationship has already survived the unbelievable. In my opinion, love like that comes only once in a lifetime. You have to think it over very carefully."

"Beth, you completed some grueling work to become a Special Agent," her father said. "No matter what, I'll support your decision."

Beth returned home feeling none the wiser and more confused than ever.

The following day was more enlightening, as she sat in front of Tony Kuertz, the ASAC for Suffolk County. Incredulous, Tony couldn't believe Beth followed Anthony to Costa Rica. Even worse, she was thinking of joining him. It was beyond Tony's comprehension.

"He's everything you have fought against for your entire career," Tony said. "He's a criminal, a con man, a fugitive from the law, a coward, someone who took advantage of the elderly, and he was considered one of the most-valuable citizens of his community."

When Beth tried to explain Anthony's situation, Tony stared in disbelief.

"Will you think about what you just said?" Tony asked. "If word gets out about any of this, your FBI career is over. You could even be breaking the law just by living with him, essentially condoning his behavior. You could be charged with aiding and abetting a crime.

"If we ever manage to extradite him, what will you do? You need to go home without saying a word about this to anyone. Come back in when you're in your right mind. I'll cover for you by saying you're ill."

That night, she called Anthony and told him she wasn't going to join him in Costa Rica. As the connection fell silent, she felt sick to her stomach. He hadn't hung up, and she could only imagine how upset he was.

"I think it's best if we don't speak again," she said, ending the call.

She wept silently when she crawled into bed. Although emotionally and physically exhausted, sleep eluded her.

Still in bed the following day, she barely ate anything. Miserable and desperately missing Anthony, she kept going over what Tony Kuertz told her, trying to convince herself she made the right decision.

She considered calling Anthony back only to decide against it.

When Tony called, she agreed to come back to work the following day.

"You've got a complicated case waiting for you that should keep your mind busy," he said.

Thirteen

The four fugitives loved Costa Rica. Phil got a job as a business consultant for a construction company based in Liberia. Joe was doing some consulting, too, along with hands-on work with a competing construction company. Business was doing well, with many hotels and apartment buildings being built near the beaches. Sam, who was bartending at a local tiki bar on the beach loved it.

Anthony set himself up as a Home Inspector for Americans and Europeans building homes or buying pre-existing homes. Once word got out that a former building inspector from the U.S. was conducting home inspections in Costa Rica, Anthony's phone wouldn't stop ringing.

Still depressed over losing Beth, he was grateful to be busy. The job allowed him to meet clients from around the world. He was good at his job, and his clients were willing to pay. It was also an opportunity to meet beautiful women. Before Beth, he would have taken advantage of that, but he was no longer interested.

Jim and Phil bought two condos on the beach within walking distance of Anthony's home. Sam opted to stay with Anthony. Daniella and the boys immediately fell in love with the country. After their first visit, they returned to Minneola and put the house on the market to sell, so they could move to Costa Rica. Anthony bought a home for them five miles away. There were many American ex-pats in the neighborhood, with an abundance of children. The boys would be happy there.

    Anthony approached his parents about the possibility they might want to move to Costa Rica, too. They replied they didn't want to leave the States, but they would visit as often as possible. Their first trip would be in four months. Anthony didn't understand why they wanted to wait so long, but there was no point in challenging them.

    Daniella sold her home within one week of listing it. Being able to sell it furnished made her life much easier. The car took longer to sell than the house. She transferred her money to the Banco Nacional, ensuring her a path toward citizenship. It was bittersweet leaving her family and friends, but she would be busy soon enough with visitors at her new home. Her parents would travel with her to Liberia to help with the twins.

    They hadn't seen the house until Anthony picked them up at the airport and drove them through the electric gate. Daniella and her parents were speechless. It was a beautiful, contemporary two-story white house with plenty of windows.

    Anthony ushered them in through the foyer and gave them the grand tour. It was difficult to believe. The house was modern but remained warm and inviting. A baby grand piano sat to one side of the great room. Looking past it, they saw a large swimming pool through the patio doors, surrounded by lush vegetation and palm trees. An elevator took them to the second floor, where ocean views were visible through floor-to-ceiling windows. Mario and Matteo had their own rooms, both decorated perfectly. The opulent master bedroom had an adjoining dressing area and large bath.

    Daniella's parents looked for the guest bedroom, and Anthony led them back to the first floor and out the patio doors to a second building also facing the pool.

"This is the guest house," he explained.

It was as lovely as the main house, with a small kitchen, two bedrooms, and a bathroom.

The boys, bored from looking around, quickly stripped to jump into the pool. Anthony stripped down to his underwear and joined them.

Daniella went into the fully stocked kitchen and brought Anthony a beer, then opened a bottle of wine for everyone else. They sat on the patio furniture and watched father and sons try to wear each other out. It was the most fun Anthony had since Beth left. He made a mental note that his life would be centered around the boys and his business.

The following weeks were incredible for Anthony, giving him plenty of time to catch up with the boys. However, the situation changed when he received a phone call from his father.

"Alfonse is in critical condition after an incident at the jail," he explained. "He hasn't been moved to Otisville yet and was still in the Suffolk County jail, where several inmates beat him nearly to death. He was taken by medical helicopter to Nassau University Medical Center.

"Alfonse's mother and wife, together with Maria, your mother, are at the hospital and will call with any updates. I'll let you know how this goes."

Many hours later, Anthony was told that Alfonse was still critical but had become stable. Over the following days, as he fought for his life, Margaret never left his side. He suffered many broken bones, including his jaw, which had to be wired shut. His kidneys suffered irrevocable damage, he had a collapsed lung, both eyes were swollen shut, and his body was bruised all over. He remained on a ventilator.

Whoever attacked him wanted him dead. As his battered body began to heal, his kidneys continued to fail. He was placed on dialysis, and Margaret learned that might be for the rest of his life.

A guard was outside Alfonse's door day and night to remind everyone Alfonse was still a prisoner. Eventually, he was moved to the trauma ICU at the Medical Center, because he had too many injuries to be kept at the correctional infirmary.

Alfonse eventually woke up, but he wasn't lucid. Although he was nonverbal, he could blink his eyes at people he recognized. The doctors explained his brain was badly injured, and it would take time to heal. He had to learn how to talk again when his brain was ready.

Both legs were broken. One had a rod inserted into the bone, and the other had an external rod. His right arm was in a cast, and his jaw was still wired shut, but the chest tube for his collapsed lung was removed. A tube in his stomach provided nutrition. He was finally taken off the ventilator and given an oxygen mask. His bruises were healing, giving him a yellowed, jaundiced look. The doctor recommended he be sent to a nursing home in a rehab facility. His case was too complicated for him to go to a prison infirmary, so he was transported to the Nassau University Medical Center Nursing Home, which allowed Margaret to remain at his side.

Once he was in rehab and had his jaw no longer wired, he began talking, slowly at first, then in complete sentences. He had full memory of the beating and was terrified it would happen again. His bones began healing well, so he spent time in the gymnasium trying to relearn how to walk. He continued his kidney dialysis, with his kidneys showing little to no improvement.

The biggest challenge was his mental state. Normally a quiet, friendly man, he became suspicious of everyone. He believed they were out to get him, including Margaret on one occasion. He was withdrawn and snapped at people who tried to talk to him. He questioned his daily medications and had an unpleasant attitude toward the nurses.

Part of his rehab focused on his mental health. Alfonse met with a psychiatrist daily. He didn't like the man and wasn't shy about saying so. Dr. Johnson told Margaret that was normal following brain trauma.

"His brain is still trying to recover, and it will be some time before he's normal again."

They spoke at length about Alfonse's career and his downfall.

"The judge sentenced him to a white-collar prison at Otisville," she said.

"He might never get there. He might remain in a prison hospital for the rest of his sentence. That would be the best for him, both for security and his well-being. I've told the medical team about his situation, and they agree. He'll remain in rehab for another month before we make our final decision."

During the final weeks of Alfonse's rehab, he made good recovery on everything except his kidneys and mental health. He woke in the middle of the night, screaming someone was in his room and wanted to kill him. Although he was given sedatives, the nightmares continued. He had kidney dialysis every other day, and he continued seeing Dr. Johnson daily.

Slowly, Alfonse's strength and stamina increased, although he still couldn't walk and had trouble grasping objects with his right hand, because nerve damage occurred with the fracture.

He began writing with his left hand once he was able to grasp the pen. It seemed as if his body was healing, yet his mental health was deteriorating.

Finally, the medical team decided to send him to the Arthur Kill Mental Health Unit at the Arthur Kill Correctional Facility on Staten Island. Dr. Johnson visited the facility once a month and would be able to see him there.

Margaret would be allowed to visit as often as she wished. That meant taking a train from Minneola, but it was doable. She was asked to stay away for the first week, so the new staff could get Alfonse on a regimen of medications and observe his response.

She went to see him the first day she could and was horrified. He lay in bed, obviously drugged, and didn't respond to her questions. She wasn't even sure he recognized her. When she asked to speak with a doctor, she was told she had to make an appointment.

When Margaret voiced her concerns to a nurse, the woman said, "He screamed bloody murder for days. This way, he can rest."

Margaret made an appointment to see the doctor the following day as well as contacting Dr. Johnson to advise him of her husband's condition. Dr. Johnson would visit the prison the following week and would assess Alfonse's condition.

Margaret finally met Dr. Ross, the physician at the prison.

"Alfonse didn't make a good transition from the hospital in Nassau. Not only is he hallucinating, he pulled out his dialysis catheter, which required an emergency transfer to the local hospital. He also assaulted a nurse by throwing a container of urine at her.

"We tried various medications to calm him, but only the sedatives achieved any semblance of calm. I understand Dr. Johnson will be here next week to assess your husband. He might require a transfer to a higher level of care."

"What facility would offer that kind of care?"

"Rikers Island."

KAREN MCSHANE

Fourteen

Maria Vito visited Beth often over the following four weeks. Beth and Maria became close, as Maria told her about Anthony's antics as a boy. Beth enjoyed hearing about how Anthony always looked after the younger boys and made sure they were included in the events of the Little Italy streets.

One Sunday, Maria brought a photo album. The three women laughed hysterically at some of the pictures. Suddenly, Beth froze, and her expression changed to horror.

Dorothy and Maria stopped laughing to look at her. Beth slowly got out of bed in total control, quietly saying, "I need to go to the hospital. My water just broke."

Six hours later, Beth was exhausted. Maria mopped her brow, as Dorothy rubbed her shoulders. Dr. Hope encouraged Beth to have an epidural, but she refused.

As hours passed, Beth remained defiant. Finally, Dr. Hope said, "You're fully dilated."

Triumphant but tired, she began pushing. All her sadness, stress, uncertainty, strength, and love for Anthony and her new daughter gave her the endurance to keep pushing until she heard the first tiny cries from Antonia Elizabeth Vito. Beth sobbed when her baby was placed on her chest.

Maria and Dorothy hugged each other and took turns photographing the mother and child. As Beth was taken to the postpartum room, Anthony Vito, Sr. and Beth's father, John, arrived to meet their new granddaughter. ASAC Tony Kuertz came in, too.

Beth and Tia returned to his parents' home with regular visits from Mari and Anthony, Sr. Beth spent many sleepless nights with Tia and was amazed how closely she resembled her father. She was a vibrant, happy baby, rarely crying who enjoyed staying awake all night to play with her mother.

As a new mother, Beth felt terrible guilt for keeping Tia's existence a secret from Anthony. How could she deprive him of this little miracle? Could she take Tia away from her stable life in the U.S.?

When Tia was three months old, Beth saw how fast she was growing and changing, and she could no longer deprive Anthony of the knowledge of his daughter.

Once Tai was cleared by the pediatrician to fly, Maria and Anthony, Sr. contacted Anthony and Sam in Costa Rica, saying they would visit soon and would need a ride from the airport.

"I'll come get you," Sam said. "Anthony isn't himself these days."

"He has to be there," Maria insisted.

Anthony begrudgingly agreed to accompany Sam to the airport but refused to shave, as Sam suggested. The two waited for the new arrivals, as JetBlue passengers flooded the arrival lounge.

Sam waved and shouted, saying he just saw Maria, but she was with a woman he didn't recognize. He saw Anthony's father, but he was also with an unfamiliar face.

Anthony's parents hugged them both, then introduced their friends, Dorothy and John.

"I didn't know you were bringing friends," Anthony said, looking confused.

"They aren't friends, Anthony," his mother said. "They're family."

Still confused, Anthony shook John's hand and gave Dorothy a quick hug.

In the embrace, Dorothy whispered something. Anthony stepped back and said, "What did you just say?"

"I'd like to introduce you to your new daughter, Antonia, and my daughter, who I believe you know—Elizabeth."

He stared, unable to comprehend her words, when Beth, carrying Tia, walked into the lounge and approached Anthony with a smile.

"Anthony, this is my mom, Dorothy, and my dad, John—and this is Antonia, your daughter."

Anthony was completely stunned. Beth passed Antonia to Maria

"Come on, Anthony," Maria said. "You'll want to remember this moment the rest of your life. This is your daughter, Tia. She's been waiting to meet you."

Beth placed Antonia into Anthony's arms, as tears streamed down his face. "Tia, this is your daddy."

"Why didn't you tell me?" Anthony whispered. "I could have taken care of you."

"I wasn't sure. It was a difficult pregnancy, and I couldn't travel. Now, I'm sure. I've never been so sure of anything in my life."

"Are you staying?"

"If you'll have us both."

He put an arm around Beth with Tia cushioned between them. "Thank you, both of you."

"Come on," Beth said with a smile. "Let's go home. Mum and Dad are staying at the local hotel."

"Why?"

"I wasn't sure if you had enough room."

"It's just Sam and me. Phil and Joe moved out six months ago to their own place. We've got plenty of room, believe me."

"Will that work for you two?" Beth asked her parents.

"Yet bet," John said. "I'm looking forward to seeing where little Tia and her mommy will live. We'll get a taxi and follow you."

"Anthony, Senior, and I will come with you. Let's pick up dinner on the way."

"I'll come, too," Sam said. "I know the best take-out places."

Anthony, Beth, and Tia walked slowly to the baggage area and collected their bags, as well as Tia's car seat.

Beth skillfully fastened the car seat in the back of Anthony's car and slipped into the front passenger seat. There was an awkward silence, as they drove away from the airport.

"Anthony," she asked quietly, "don't you want us here?"

"Of course I do, but what kind of life will you two have? You'll be living with a fugitive in a foreign country. What about your career and Tia's future?"

"I've had nine long months of bed rest to come to this decision. I did my homework. There's an American school Tia can attend. When I'm ready to go back to work, believe me, the Costa Rican government will be eager to give me a job. Raising our child in a beautiful tropical country seems like a good deal to me. Raising her in a two-parent family is even better. Damn, I won't even miss the snow."

"I can't believe this is happening. I had no idea." He fought back tears. "I thought I'd never see you again. Now you're sitting beside me, and our daughter is in the back. It's almost too much."

"Just wait until she wants to play at three in the morning. It'll become real very quickly." She smiled and turned to see Tia falling asleep in the car. "Are you ready for your life to be turned upside down?"

He smiled. "More than you'll ever know."

Tia was still asleep, as Beth lifted her from the car to sit in her daddy's arms, her head resting against his shoulder. Tia continued sleeping, as Sam, Maria, Dorothy, John, and Anthony, Senior, arrived with paper bags of food that smelled heavenly.

Sam quickly got out plates and silverware and set the table on the lanai overlooking the pool. He quickly brought out various wines and glasses.

The commotion finally woke Tia, and she sat on Maria's lap, as Beth discussed placing a child fence around the pool with Anthony.

As Beth and Anthony lay in bed together, Tia was in a makeshift crib on the floor. Beth was delighted to discover Amazon had delivery service in Costa Rica. She already scheduled a delivery for the following day of every kind of device, furniture, and baby food, anything an American child could want, including a crib. She promised Anthony in the future, she would immerse herself in Costa Rican culture and use Amazon only when desperate.

Beth never saw her parents have so much fun before. Her dad loved swimming laps in the pool, Maria and Dorothy drank mimosas nearby, and Anthony, Senior, and Sam took walks on the beach.

Soon, Phil and John joined them. Beth took them aside to tell them about being at their mother's side when she passed away over a year earlier. She collected their mother's personal belongings and Bible from the bedside table and gave them to the men.

They were overcome with gratitude to know she hadn't died alone. Their quiet, reflective moment was soon disrupted by the sound of a baby crying. They followed Beth, as she went to scoop up her daughter and console her.

"Tia, this is Uncle Phil and Uncle Joe." She moved from side-to-side, trying to stop Tia from crying.

Anthony walked over and took Tia in his arms.

"Surprise!" he said with a smile. "This is our daughter, Antonia, or Tia for short."

"Jesus," Phil said. "What else did we miss? Didn't we see you last week? Why didn't you tell us?"

"I didn't know until yesterday. I went to pick up Mom and Dad from the airport, and, well, you can figure out the rest. This is John and Dorothy, Beth's parents."

Tia finally stopped wailing and played with Phil's beard, as he held her in his arms.

Adding to the bedlam, the five-year-old twins, Matteo and Mario, ran into the room, closely followed by their mother, Daniella. She was in the middle of telling the boys to stop running when she froze at seeing the crowd in Anthony's kitchen. She tried to process who they were when her eyes suddenly saw Beth, then Tia in Phil's arms.

Anthony carried Tia to Daniella and introduced her. She quickly lifted the baby and walked over to Beth.

"Holy cow, and congratulations, Beth! Boy, you're a dark horse. I hope there are no more surprises. Anyway, I really hope you and Tia will be staying. Anthony's been miserable without you., In fact, he's been a royal pain. Who are all these other people?"

By late afternoon, the guests finally left. John and Dorothy took a siesta, while Maria and Anthony, Senior, sat on the beach, leaving Anthony, Beth, and Tia alone.

"What is your immigration status?" Beth asked. "I have a return ticket to the States, because I don't qualify to remain in Costa Rica due to my lack of income."

"I'm a permanent resident now, and I'm on the way to naturalization. You need a monthly income of $2,500 to remain here, or at least $60,000 in a Costa Rican bank. If you marry me, as long as you're in the country for two years, you could become a naturalized citizen."

"What are you saying?" she asked coyly.

He repeated himself, which made her roll her eyes. Suddenly, it clicked.

He went to one knee and took her hand. "Beth, I loved you since the first day I saw you. It was the day you rescued my dry cleaning ticket, broke the heel of your shoe, and decided to hobble away without seeing me. I loved you when you met my family and asked if every female was named Maria. I even loved you when you tried to have me arrested, as you set me free from the disaster I created. I loved you in that ridiculous hat you used to disguise yourself when you first came to Costa Rica. Now, my darling, I love you and our beautiful little girl, Antonia, and I would be honored if you would be my wife."

Beth placed her hands on his cheeks and helped him to his feet. "Marrying you would make me complete. I love you more than I can put into words. Yes, I'll be your wife."

The following day, they left Tia with her grandparents and drove to Liberia to choose an engagement ring and wedding band.

Because a marriage license wasn't required in Costa Rica, they visited Attorney Miguel Castillo, Anthony's lawyer and friend.

"Welcome back to Costa Rica," he said. "I knew you'd come back, but you sure took your time."

"Miguel," Anthony said, "we're engaged. I'd like you to come to my house on Saturday to perform the marriage ceremony. I'd also like you to handle her immigration paperwork. I'll give Beth $60,000 to open a bank account in her name."

Beth returned to Liberia the following day with her mother, Maria Vito, and Daniella Vito. They were looking for a dress for Beth and something for Tia, who was back at home with the men and her stepbrothers, Mario and Matteo.

During the trip to town, Beth received a call from Tony Kuertz.

"I'm just checking in," Tony said, "but I received a call from Dorothy McLeary yesterday, so I know about your impending wedding. Congratulations! Unfortunately, it would be suicide for my career if I attended."

While Beth was on bed rest during her pregnancy, she was technically on sick leave, then she had maternity leave after Antonia was born. Before she left to come back to Costa Rica, she submitted her resignation by mail to the Melville office, which Tony advised her to do.

Beth, with her father carrying Tia, walked down the sand aisle strewn with pink bougainvillea to a circle of people near waves lapping at the shore. The circle opened to reveal Anthony in the center, wearing cream cotton slacks and a cream shirt. Beth and Tia wore matching cream dresses.

Beth and Tia joined Anthony in the center of the circle, as her father joined her mother. Attorney Miguel Castillo stood before them to conduct the ceremony.

Beth turned and gave Tia to Anthony's mother, then she held Anthony's hands in hers. The ceremony was short but very meaningful. They exchanged vows and were pronounced man and wife, as the sun set over the horizon.

The party moved to the swimming pool area at the house, where a steel drum band played, and a local restaurateur prepared a traditional Costa Rican wedding dinner for them.

Beth and Anthony had their first dance as husband and wife, then the party began, continuing until the early morning. Both sets of parents retired at midnight, with John and Dorothy taking a very sleepy Tia with them.

After the music stopped, and everyone retired to their rooms, Beth and Anthony walked along the beach hand-in-hand.

"If you asked me ten years ago where I'd be today," Beth said, "I could never have predicted this."

He smiled. "You mean falling in love, having a child with a fugitive felon who you wanted to send to jail, then marrying said criminal and living on the beach in tropical Costa Rica? What's the big deal?"

"Well, when you put it like that...." She began laughing.

"I love you, Mrs. Vito." He took her in his arms. "I love all three of us. I never knew I could be so happy."

Beth smiled and kissed him gently.

Fifteen

Alfonse became a patient in the mental health hospital at Rikers Island Correctional Facility. Dr. Johnson assessed him at the Arthur Kill facility and deemed he needed a higher-level treatment facility. He knew several colleagues at the Rikers Island location and assured Margaret it was the right move for Alfonse.

She wasn't allowed to see Alfonse for the first month, to give him time to be stabilized.

She was glad to hear from Dr. Jackson at Rikers Island, who called to say, "He's responding well to treatment. He's no longer sedated and is in therapy, and I feel he would benefit by a visit from you."

The following day, she took the train and met Dr. Jackson.

"Recent tests have shown that Alfonse had a stroke at the time of his assault in the jail," Dr. Jackson said. "With all the swelling in his brain, the medical team couldn't visualize the stroke, but this helps explain the continued weakness in his right arm and other deficits. Due to the stroke, he has lost sight in his right eye.

"His treatment now focuses on physical therapy for those deficits, speech therapy, and therapeutic medication for depression and paranoia."

Just before they left the consultation room, Dr. Jackson dropped his pen. As he stooped over to pick it up, he whispered,

"You may want to speak to your attorney about the challenges Alfonse faces." He gave her his business card.

Alfonse was in his own room in a hospital bed, with a large red sign above the bed that read *Fall Risk*. He was dozing, as she sat beside the bed, softly stroking his forehead until he opened his eyes.

He smiled in recognition, although only the left side of his mouth moved. He took her hand and kissed it gently.

"I know you can't talk yet, so please nod if you understand me."

He nodded.

She explained what Dr. Jackson told her, and he nodded to indicate he knew about it.

"I'll do everything in my power to get you the best treatment. Don't lose hope."

He smiled.

She explained how the family was doing, although she wasn't sure how he would take the news that the FBI agent who arrested him just had Anthony's baby, so she left that out.

After thirty minutes, he began dozing. She promised to visit him as soon as she could.

When Margaret left Rikers Island, she immediately called her attorney and told him what Dr. Jackson said.

"This is way over my head," the attorney replied. "I'll pass this on to a friend who works on the Compassionate Release Program within the Federal Bureau of Prisons. I'll be in touch."

When Margaret arrived home, she found a message waiting on her home phone from Attorney John White, telling her to call him on his cell.

For the next hour, she filled Attorney White in on the case against Alfonse and the devastating assault he suffered at the jail before his scheduled move to Otisville Correctional Facility. She added what Dr. Jackson told her and gave the attorney his number.

"Under the Compassionate Release Program, a prisoner suffering from a debilitating and incurable medical condition, where the prisoner is unable to care for himself, may be considered for early release. That fact that the condition was inflicted on him while he was in custody will help the case. I'll do some research and will be in touch after I have spoken to Dr. Jackson and Dr. Johnson. I work these cases pro bono. I must caution you not to get your hopes up. This is a long process, and it's an emotional rollercoaster. You need to line up as many people as you can to vouch for your husband to attest to what kind of person he was before the crime was committed. That always helps."

Margaret had a mission. She visited Alfonse three times a week and often arrived while he was in speech therapy, which he took in the hope of being able to speak again. His comprehension was perfect, but he couldn't verbalize his answers. He was also in physical therapy to build up his strength. Because he couldn't bear any weight on his right arm, he was confined to a wheelchair. Though weak, his right arm grew stronger daily with weight-bearing exercises, but his motor function in that arm was still poor.

While he was in therapy, she saw the old Alfonse and his determination, although when he was taken back to his hospital room, he retreated into sadness she never saw in him before. She didn't tell him about the Compassionate Release Program, because she didn't want to raise false hopes. To brighten his spirits, she brought in the local newspaper and read stories to him.

Working through Attorney White, Margaret started a petition to release Alfonse from prison on compassionate grounds. She received hundreds of letters from fellow officers in the police force describing the impact Alfonse made on their lives.

After a local newspaper featured her story, she received more letters from all over the country containing stories about how Alfonse changed their lives. She even heard from people abroad about similar cases that warranted release from incarceration on grounds of compassion.

Although Margaret didn't ask for money, it poured in. With Attorney White's help, she opened an account to help all inmates who qualified for the Compassionate Release Program. As local congressmen heard about Alfonse, they added their support, and soon Senators from New York State and surrounding states added their voices.

After six months of intense work by Attorney White, an application for medical parole was filed stating that Alfonse had a significant, debilitating illness that was permanent but non-terminal. His condition made him physically and cognitively no threat to society.

The application was sent to the Commissioner of the New York Department of Corrections, along with a copy to the Department's Division of Health Services. Accompanying the application were reports from various doctors within Rikers Health Department who agreed with the prognosis. Also included were statements from the general public and former colleagues of Alfonse, stating how he helped them individually and how he served his country in the military and then as a policeman.

They didn't receive a reply for four agonizing weeks. Finally, the Commissioner initiated a medical investigation into Alfonse's case together with a discharge/exit plan for his parole.

Then it was the turn of a physician within the Rikers Island Department of Health to evaluate the prisoner to determine that all eligibility criteria were met. Margaret and Attorney White were ecstatic when they learned that the evaluating physician would be Dr. Jackson.

Within fourteen days, Dr. Jackson referred his findings to the Commissioner, the Deputy Commissioner, the Chief Medical Officer, and the Medical Parole Coordinator for a decision.

After a further two weeks, the Commissioner determined that the criteria of a debilitating medical condition was met, together with the fact that Alfonse was no threat to society. The paperwork was forwarded to the New York Board of Parole.

At that stage, the real work of releasing Alfonse began. It had to be determined where and how he would be transferred, who would provide his medication, and who would provide his ongoing physical and occupational therapy, as well as who would pay for his treatment.

Margaret requested he be transferred back home, because Alfonse's insurance would provide for a home nurse and aid to assist in his daily living activities. A social worker from the Office of Victim Assistance visited Margaret at home to see how Alfonse would be cared for and whether the house was a safe environment for him. Happy with her findings, she recommended Alfonse be paroled to home.

The Offender Rehabilitation Program Director also contacted Margaret to discuss Alfonse's post parole requirements.

"Before the six-month mark of your husband's post release, another physician's report will be needed to prove he is still eligible for medical parole. The report must be sent to the New York Board of Parole, which will then grant another six months of medical parole."

Finally, the day of Alfonse's release arrived. The Office of Victim Assistance arranged an ambulance to bring him home. He still didn't know that Margaret and the attorney managed to get his compassionate release approved.

Margaret arrived at the hospital and sat on Alfonse's bed. He smiled and took her hand in his left hand.

"Alfonse, listen carefully."

He nodded.

"You're finally going home."

He nodded and shrugged, not believing her.

"It's taken us twelve months of hard work. We have dozens of letters of support from people around the world." Tears filled her eyes. "Hundreds of people wrote to the Commissioner to tell them how you helped them. You meet the criteria for compassionate release, and you are, indeed, coming home."

His eyes grew wider and wider.

Dr. Jackson walked in and asked, "Are you ready to leave?"

"Dr. Jackson played a huge role in getting you released," she told Alfonse.

He began crying and sobbing uncontrollably. Margaret cradled his head in her arms and whispered, "The nightmare is almost over."

Sixteen

Family life for Anthony, Beth, and Tia meant Anthony worked Monday through Friday, while Beth stayed home to raise their daughter. She enrolled Tia in an American school, and she was allowed to start classes at their morning preschool program once she turned four. Anthony dropped her off each morning on his way to work, because Beth, pregnant with their second child, battled morning sickness.

Talks between the U.S. and Costa Rican meant an improvement in relations as well as extraditions. Although Anthony, Beth, and Tia were Costa Rican citizens, that didn't stop the U.S. media from trying to interview them about their escape from U.S. custody. They followed Beth regularly, and it was increasingly difficult to get away from the car tailing her when she drove to Tia's school.

Back in the U.S., Beth's parents saw Anthony's story featured on a Sunday-night TV news show. Beth worried Costa Rican authorities would eventually be pressured into extraditing Anthony back to the United States. Even their attorney, Miguel Castillo, couldn't guarantee their safety anymore.

Anthony and Beth knew moving to a non-extradition country with the United States would be impossible, especially with Beth pregnant. The majority of those countries were in Africa, the

United Arab Emirates, and Vietnam, and were difficult to travel to and even more difficult to establish citizenship.

After more research, they learned of certain countries that still refused extradition requests, including Cuba, Bolivia, and Ecuador. Of them all, Ecuador was the closest and easiest to reach. It also boasted a high standard of affordable health care, a low cost of living, low unemployment, and great year-round weather. Ecuador was home to a large population of U.S. expats and international schools. Visas were easy to obtain, with citizenship available after three years.

Ecuador also suffered from natural disasters, including earthquakes, volcanoes, and landslides. With Anthony in construction, he would have to investigate any potential property to ensure they would be safe. At that point, though, they had little choice. To avoid the sleeping volcanoes and fault lines running through the country, they decided to move to the coastal town of Manta.

Anthony sat around the large dining room table, outlining their plans to Daniella, Sam, Phil, and Joe. All agreed Anthony should go to Ecuador first with Attorney Miguel Castillo to find a home for the family. Once settled, if any of the others wanted to join them, they would be welcome. Miguel would sell the house in Costa Rica for them after they were settled in Ecuador to avoid alerting anyone of their whereabouts, including members of the media.

The week prior to Anthony's leaving for Ecuador, they had devastating news from home. Alfonse suffered a massive, fatal stroke while sleeping. Margaret checked on him earlier that morning, and he looked so peaceful she decided to let him sleep an extra hour.

Everyone was devastated by the news, but Anthony took it the hardest. Alfonse had always been his mentor, the one who did the right thing. He remained in America to face his crimes, and Anthony knew it was his fault Alfonse got involved in illegal activities. He felt responsible for Alfonse's death.

Arrangements were made for the funeral the same day Anthony would travel to Ecuador. For the next few days, Anthony, miserable in grief, didn't eat, sleep, or talk.

Finally, Beth sat him down and said, "Alfonse would never want you to act this way."

She held his head in both hands, as he sobbed. When he finally calmed, he called Margaret, Alfonse's wife, and spoke with her at length. She repeated what Beth told him, and he returned to work the following day.

The day of the funeral, Beth drove a somber Anthony to the airport. Miguel arranged a private jet to take him to Porto Viejo, Ecuador, where they would obtain visas and meet with the bank manager of the Banco Pichincha. Miguel opened accounts there in Anthony's name and transferred funds the previous day. Once finished with the paperwork, they would drive twenty-three miles to the town of Manta on the Pacific Ocean. Known as the tuna capital of the world, it was home to a very large, colorful fishing fleet. They would tour homes for the next two days with a Realtor.

Once they were airborne, Miguel presented Anthony with a large glass of whiskey and encouraged him to talk about his cousin. Each time he tried, Anthony broke down into tears. They sat in silence, the hum of the plane and the effect of the whiskey lulling Anthony to sleep. Knowing Anthony hadn't been sleeping well, Miguel let him rest the entire flight.

Anthony woke to the jolt of their wheels touching down on tarmac. They deplaned and cleared customs quickly, completing the final portion of the visas requirement with the help of an English-speaking customs officer. Miguel arranged for a car to take them to the Banco Pichincha to meet Alejandro Sanchez, the manager.

Mr. Sanchez was short in stature and big in personality. He welcomed them both with hugs and ushered them into his office, introducing them to his staff along the way, as if they were celebrities. He told them he arranged for a traditional Ecuadorian lunch after the formalities.

By the time Anthony and Miguel arrived in Manta, the sun was setting. They were exhausted, as they went to their rooms at a local hotel after agreeing to meet in the morning.

Anthony called Beth to check in before settling in for the night. He heard Tia in the background, giggling and playing with her toys. He longed to be with them, but it also made him more determined to find a stable, safe environment for them to live.

The Realtor had six homes and two condominiums on the schedule for them. Anthony didn't want to live in a condo with a four-year-old and a new baby, so he deleted those from the schedule immediately. His knowledge of home construction enabled him to eliminate two of the homes quickly, and location eliminated two others, leaving two as contenders. Both were on the beach.

The first, Casa Mondela, was a more-traditional Ecuadorian home, boasting dark woods and a large stone fireplace with a Spanish flair on the exterior. The home was fifty years old but had been well constructed and maintained.

The second home was the total opposite—brand new, contemporary, furnished, with five bedrooms, nine bathrooms, a heated pool, outdoor kitchen, and was luxurious from every standpoint, built by an American to American standards.

Anthony made arrangements to see both homes again the following day and spoke to Beth about them over the phone. They agreed Anthony would FaceTime her to show the homes, but Beth could tell he was in favor of the new, furnished, contemporary house.

Seventeen

Even though they would be selling their beautiful furnished home in Playa Conchal, Beth was surprised by how many personal possessions they accumulated during the last four years. Anthony was already living in Manta, while Beth finished packing boxes to be transported to Ecuador by private charter plane arranged by Miguel.

Sam, Phil, and Joe would accompany her, so they could see the country. Phil and Joe were recently featured in an American news program, so they seriously considered the move. Anthony made arrangements for them to meet his new best friend, Alejandro Sanchez, from the bank, and the new house was big enough for them to live until they found their own homes.

Daniella would be the only one remaining in Playa Conchal. Remarried and very happy, she didn't want to move any farther south.

Tia kept everyone occupied during the two-and-a-half-hour flight to Porto Viejo, Ecuador, and promptly fell asleep when they landed. Anthony met them as soon as they cleared customs.

Joe and Phil rented a car, and Anthony brought the new SUV to help carry all the luggage, Tia's booster seat, and the passengers. They convoyed down to the coastal town of Manta.

Traffic was light, so they arrived in less than an hour. Anthony used the remote to open the wrought-iron gates to their new home. As they drove through, Beth gasped, because FaceTime hadn't done the place justice. It was a stunning house, a white modern structure with large glass windows, elegant pillars, and marble accents, all framed with beautiful manicured gardens and water features.

The cars parked in front of three garage doors. Mesmerized, Beth stepped from the car and walked to the rear of the home. A large swimming pool spilled over a wall to recycle the water into a large spa. An outdoor kitchen and relaxation area with marble accents sat to the side of the pool, with hammocks and a large outdoor dining table to welcome the guests. Balconies wrapped around each of the three floors, complete with lounge chairs and umbrellas.

Anthony appeared at the glass doors. "Come inside!" he called.

She continued the tour, with Tia holding her hand. The more she saw, the more she loved it. Finally, they returned to the kitchen, where Anthony poured wine glasses for all of them.

He turned to Beth and asked nervously, "Well?"

"I would say I love it, but it's more than that. This is incredible. I couldn't be happier. Thank you!" Putting her arms around him, she kissed him. "Good job," she whispered.

The following morning, they left in their respective cars after breakfast. Anthony took Sam, Beth, and Tia on a tour of the area, while Joe and Phil met a Realtor for a house tour. Anthony would take them to meet Alejandro Sanchez at the bank the following day. Sam would move in with Anthony and Beth until he found a job in Manta. He would get his own accommodations later.

The first week was a flurry of activity for Beth, unpacking, organizing, and entertaining Phil and Joe. The hardest thing was figuring out which light switch operated which light. The rest of their possessions arrived by truck and were unloaded into one of the three garages. Beth would tackle that job after Phil and Joe left.

The other priority was finding a school for Tia. There were several international schools and colleges in Manta, all with excellent reputations. Beth was pleasantly surprised to discover the large number of expats from the U.S. living in the country.

Beth found Manta was an energetic city. People were warm and friendly, and life was similar to that in the States. A new shopping mall just opened, similar to malls back home, and new projects were being built everywhere. A new museum was under construction, and the local airport was hoping to become a gateway to the Galapagos Islands. Improvements in infrastructure were being planned to draw in new business from around the world. It was a safe place to live, and the young family often walked to restaurants along the harbor for dinner in the evening.

As much as Beth loved living in Costa Rica, she flourished in Ecuador. She made many friends, as did Anthony and Tia. Phil and Joe settled quickly, too. With Anthony, they began a new business consulting for Americans moving to Ecuador. They converted existing homes, bringing them up to American standard workmanship, as well as contracting for new construction that could withstand sizeable earthquakes. They were soon inundated with work but were very careful not to take on more than they could handle.

Both men began dating, and, for the first time in years, they were planning for the future.

Beth's second pregnancy was totally different from her first, bedridden one. Once she got through the first trimester of morning sickness, she was completely healthy. She registered with an American obstetrician who assured her that her pregnancy was progressing well. An ultrasound at three months confirmed they were expecting a son. Beth suggested the name of John Anthony Vito.

John Anthony Vito made an unexpected entrance into the world in the back of his daddy's car on the way to the hospital. Beth's water broke, as she prepared dinner one evening. With Tia's birth, it was hours after her water broke before Tia made her appearance, so Beth went on preparing dinner for her family and Sam, even though her contractions were coming close together.

By the time they ate, said good-bye, and left for the hospital, Beth knew she was in trouble. As she panted loudly, she said, "Pull over!"

Before Anthony could stop and run around to the passenger side, baby John entered the world. Anthony held him gently, as he took his first cries, placing him on Beth's chest before driving the rest of the way, laughing and crying.

The following morning, Tia and Beth cuddled in Beth's hospital bed, and Anthony held baby John. Beth looked at her family and couldn't believe how happy she was. Who would have thought she would fall in love with and marry a man on the run from the law, the same law she swore to uphold? With Anthony, she walked away from a career she loved, left her parents and family, absconded from the United States to Costa Rica, then Ecuador, and just gave birth to their second child.

She had everything she needed except for one thing. She wanted to know if the last domino had fallen.

This is Karen McShane's debut novel

Milton Keynes UK
Ingram Content Group UK Ltd.
UKHW020603161123
432678UK00001B/2

9 781892 986528